ORANGEY 2

BY

COLIN PARKER

Haggotty & Spooks

A catalogue record of this book is available from the British Library

First Edition: September 2010

ISBN: 978-1-84375-605-7

To order additional copies of this book please visit:
http://www.prestige-press.com/colinparker

Published by: Prestige Press
Email: info@prestige-press.com
Web: http://www.prestige-press.com

Best Wishes

[signature]

December 2010.

ORANGEY 2

BY

COLIN PARKER

PRESTIGE PRESS

CONTENTS

ORANGEY AND THE LOST GHOST

It was during the summer holidays, while Orangey and Goldie were lying by the waterfall, trying to count the number of sparkling trout who were leaping for flies in the bright sunlight. The pair soon lost count and lay on the bank chatting and enjoying the warm sunshine.

Orangey's brothers Bluey, Greeny and Pinky were playing games further down the river where the water was deeper. "Pretending to be pirates I expect", thought Orangey, as even little elves love pretend games. Of course to ordinary people they looked just like any other boy or girl, but really they were mischievous elves, which gave them the chance to engage in exciting adventures at night. Sometimes just meeting the fairies in the wood, but often dodging the wicked old witch Haggotty, and keeping clear of her crazy cat Spooks.

Orangey and his cousin Goldie were both just a trifle different, as they both possessed special magic powers. As most of you know already Orangey is a 'magic elf', and Goldie an elphine who also shares an extraordinary magic influence with which they have to be very careful, so as not to alarm grownups.

Suddenly something made them both look up, and they noticed a dim flickering light, hovering above the river. Then slowly the air around them became strangely cold making them shiver. The light stopped right in front of their eyes, then slowly deepened into the shape of a hooded man. He looked at them through his dull sunken eyes, the massive bunch of ancient iron keys dangling from his thick brown leather belt, clanged together as he spoke. His voice was surprisingly soothing and lyrical, "Don't be afraid my children", he intoned, "I'm looking for my house, although I fear I've lost it after haunting it for over four hundred years". He cleared his throat huskily and spoke a little louder, "You see it was down by a river, and when I died I refused to leave it, I continued to walk the corridors for centuries, keeping a lookout in case my enemies should return and attack my family again".

Recovering from his surprise at seeing a ghost materialise right in front of them, Orangey asked, "Where was your house situated, we don't know of one near here?".

"I'm afraid that is part of the problem", replied the ghost, "You see I sometimes sleep for many years at a time, and this time when I awoke, my house had vanished". His shoulders sagged as he continued speaking, "Every tile, beam, door and window has been spirited away". His head sank into his chest, "What can I do?" he wailed. Orangey thought that he could be crying. "Well cheer up", suggested Orangey brightly, "we'll help you find it". The ghost peered at them through misty eyes wet with tears, "Would you?" he whispered.

"If you meet us tonight by this waterfall, we'll bring my brothers, and the fairies will help search too", assured Orangey. The ghost sighed with relief, and disappeared leaving a chill in the summer air. The forest suddenly seemed darker, and the smaller animals ran for their hideaways shivering with a fear they did not understand.

That night a heavy mist was rising off the forest making the undergrowth dank and odorous, as Orangey and his brothers flew down the river to the meeting place. Sensibly they had waited until their father and mother along with most other people had gone to bed, before they left the house. They had flown secretly out of the bedroom window into the awaiting forest. As they arrived at the waterfall and landed near the two old oak trees, they saw that Goldie was already sitting there, just away from the spilling waterfall. It was an extremely hot night and they enjoyed the light spray splashing on them from the falling water. They huddled together expectantly waiting to hear the tale of the lost ghost. Rapidly Orangey and Goldie explained about the meeting with the lost spirit, and how worried and sad he looked. "Where is he now?" asked Bluey, glancing round nervously. "Are you sure that it's safe here?" added Pinky with an anxious shrug.

Before there was any reply, a cold cruel wind blew out from under the trees, the atmosphere around became icy cold, the droplets from the waterfall stinging them like pellets of frozen rain as they fell.

Slowly the ghost materialised, his hooded head with so sad

eyes first, then followed by the remainder of his body. The metal keys jangling on the leather belt, sounding eerily akin to chains being dragged along an empty corridor of a dungeon. Now that it was dark, his body appeared to be more substantial, which made him look altogether more frightening.

But as he spoke his deep mellow voice soothed away their fears, "My friends" he chanted, "thank you for coming". From under his cloak he pulled out an old map, yellowed with age, and held it out for them to read. They peered in the semi-darkness, the faint writing difficult to read in its old English style. "There" snapped the ghost, stabbing his finger into the centre of the map. They craned forward, screwing up their eyes and could just make out some writing ...ierehur... House, London 73 ...iles, Wine ...ter, then a squiggle and the faint word miles again.

"This is silly", insisted Goldie, "it's so dark we can't decipher it properly". She then pulled a torch from her pocket, the exceptionally bright beam dazzled them for a moment. "That's really amazingly bright" said Greeny, "Where did you get it?". "It's actually a moonbeam", replied Goldie, "It's so useful in finding my way home at night through this dark forest".

With the additional light they all eagerly scanned the map anew. "My memory must be going", uttered the ghost. "Of course my family seat was Pierehurst House, with London to the east and Winchester to the south west". "That must be it", said Orangey pointing, "Look there are other letters missing from here and there". "No small wonder after all these years", continued the ghost, "My house was situated on a low hill, with a river at the bottom, and a wood with huge oak trees on either side. It should be easy to spot". "That's really quite remarkable", said Orangey, "I thought it might be that particular house". "How could you know, it's so far away?" asked the ghost. "Well you see", Orangey replied, "Our father is a gardener, and he collects books of old houses, especially those with magnificent gardens, some date back hundreds of years".

The ghost waited impatiently as Orangey continued, "He showed me one recently, and considered it had the most glorious gardens he had ever seen, and what's more, I now remember it was called Pierehurst House". The ghost pursed his lips and asked "How does that help if you don't know where it is?". "Well you see", Orangey replied, "tomorrow I'll look up the old books in father's library and find out exactly where it is". The ghost spoke softly, "I'm afraid I can't wait until tomorrow, cannot we go to your house tonight?". "I suppose we can" said Orangey, "I'll dash back immediately and see what I can find out". "I'll follow you", the ghost said, and then abruptly vanished.

Goldie yawned, "I'm tired, I think I'll go home to bed and meet you all tomorrow to hear the latest news". The brothers decided to return home as well, as they felt there was nothing further they could do, and they were still rather afraid of the ghost. It had rather scared them the way he had disappeared so quickly without any warning, and they wondered where he was.

Orangey quickly sped home after waving goodbye to the

others, and quietly crept into the front room, the boards creaked alarmingly, and as he stood there listening, a voice boomed in the darkness. "Come now, where can we find the book?". Orangey shuddered slightly as he spied the ghost standing near the window, and as he moved the air chilled and there was a smell of rusty iron mingled with old leather that had been left out in the rain.

Orangey began searching through the larger books, and quickly found the correct volume. He turned the pages until he saw the heading in full colour, Pierehurst House, Lambtons Wood, Hunterscombe.

He turned to find the ghost looking over his shoulder, "There", said Orangey pointing to the page, "Does that ring a bell?". The ghost sucked in his breath, his voice was low and sad, "Yes", he replied, "it's my family home, but I still don't know how to find it". "Don't worry", said Orangey, "I can find it easily. My friend Caramilla the leader of the fairies related to me the whole tale of Lambtons Wood". He lowered his voice and continued, "It appears that many years ago a battle was fought there and eventually won by a knight called Piere. It was claimed that he bore a magic sword fashioned by the fairies, and that if the sword was ever lost, the family would lose their house and lands". The ghost hesitated before saying "I believe I was that Piere, and after the battle the sword did go missing, perhaps that's the reason for my many misfortunes". He wiped away a tear. "Anyway lead me there, I'll follow, and will soon be able to tell you if it is my lost house".

Realising that it was not too long until the morning,

Orangey

Orangey flew off as fast as he could, hoping that the ghost could keep up with him. However as fast as he sped, he could sense the ghost right alongside. Out of the house, over the forest, down along the flowing river, finally turning left over some low hills, flying steadily westwards.

Far in the distance Orangey noticed thin streaks of yellow and orange lights in the still dark sky, signs it would not be long before the sun showed its face.

They reached another slowly winding river, and around a long looping bend, they could see a rounded hilltop, and on either side a green wood. "This I believe is the place", whispered Orangey to the air, "I sincerely hope so", boomed an excited voice in reply, "but I can't see a house". Orangey looked down to the bottom of the hill, he was sure it was the right place, but he had to agree there was no sign of a building.

They searched the hill on both sides, they even walked around it, but there were no buildings to be seen.

Eventually they sat down under a leafy tree, with the shafts of sunlight already breaking through lighting up the colours of the wild flowers and shrubs. "I'm sorry", said Orangey, "I'll have to leave soon or I'll be late for school". The ghost sighed and his outline dimmed until he was almost invisible, "Thank you for trying I'll have to ..." his voice trailed away, and Orangey found that he was alone.

That day at school, Orangey found it extremely difficult to concentrate. The deputy head mistress, Miss Timson-Jones, shouted at him several times to wake up. He was lucky not to be made to stay behind after class, but for once Miss Timson-Jones was in a lenient mood. So he returned home at the usual time, and waited impatiently for his father to come home from work, and finish his tea.

Orangey awaited his opportunity to ask him about the historic house at Lambton's Wood, which was featured in the book.

His father slowly took out his pipe, filled it lovingly, and placed it in his mouth without lighting it. He nodded and spoke with feeling, "Beautiful old building that, late Tudor, with truly magnificent gardens, virtually the only one like it in the country".

"Why did they knock it down?" asked Orangey. "What makes you think they did?" replied his father lighting his pipe. Orangey could hardly tell him that he had visited there with a four hundred year old ghost, and they had found nothing. So he said, "I thought I read something about it", hoping his father would provide him with a clue to its present whereabouts.

"You are partially correct", his father replied, "It was removed stone by stone, timber by timber, and rebuilt at Elton Wesley, only twenty-five miles from here as a matter of fact". He added, "Mind you they could never reproduce the gardens, although they tried their level best".

Orangey was now hopping from foot to foot, dying to rush off and relate this important news to the ghost. However he resisted the temptation and asked, "Why would they move an ancient house only fifty or sixty miles?".

His father settled back in his chair enjoying Orangey's interest, but not knowing what was at the bottom of it. "I'm afraid it was the only suitable site that they could find that was in any way like the original location", his father replied.

He puffed a huge cloud of pungent smoke out into the air above Orangey's head and continued the story. "You see after a survey a few years back, they found that the land under the foundations was eroding at an exceptionally rapid rate, and they were afraid it would collapse and be lost for ever". He puffed again, this time Orangey dodged the cloud and waited for the conclusion which he felt could not be far away. "I'm glad to say that they did save it, and now beautifully restored it's open for viewing, if you and your brothers are interested, I'll take you all to see it one day quite soon".

After supper the boys scampered up to bed, whispering and asking questions about the ghost, and what had happened. Orangey explained to them all that had taken place, and added, "We must contact the ghost as soon as possible, so that I can guide him to the new location".

Bluey suddenly piped up, "It might be quite a problem to find him. We don't know where he went after he left you. He could be anywhere". Orangey agreed but with no other plan coming to mind, they flew into the forest around midnight straight to the fairies' magic circle to ask them to help in the search for the ghost. An old owl hovered overhead listing to what was going on, and set out to search for himself. When they reached the magic circle, the fairies led by Caramilla, readily agreed to help in their-search. A flash of lightening made them look anxiously at the sky and notice that the clouds were building up for a storm. It was another hot night but the black and threatening clouds promised a violent downpour at any moment, the dark skies adding a gloomy and sinister feel to the forest.

They were all a little afraid of going alone into the forest to find the ghost, so they paired off, Bluey, Greeny and Pinky all choosing their favourites, which included Cyani and Evangeline, meanwhile Orangey and Caramilla decided to search together.

Noticing the owl returning overhead, they asked for his news, but for once he'd seen nothing. Continuing through the forest they spied a squirrel in his usual hurry to collect nuts, but in reply to their question, he replied he certainly hadn't seen a ghost and what's more, didn't want to.

The deer and rabbits being so timid were frightened by even the idea of a ghost, and were really of no help, standing trembling in fear. The brothers and fairies searched diligently along the mossy banks, and could find no trace of the ghost, so decided to walk among the trees; they heard twigs snapping under their feet, which until they realised what they were, gave them a few heart-stopping moments. Once Pinky and the fairy Evangeline heard a faint rustling in the undergrowth and a huge white shape flew out of the bushes, straight at them. Evangeline opened her mouth to scream and Pinky held his breath, but it was only a wild goose. "Wow" whispered Pinky, "for a second I thought it was the ghost".

After a long and tiring search they joined forces again at

the magic circle, and sunk down tired and disheartened. "It's no use", said Greeny, "I think he's given up and gone off to sleep for the next hundred years or so".

"You may be right", Orangey reluctantly admitted, but the thought of the ghost's unhappy face made him want to keep trying. "It's impossible. He doesn't sleep anywhere near here. We've never seen him in the forest, except by the waterfall". He looked up as a few first drops of rain pattered on the dead leaves, and added, "If he has gone to his secret sleeping place, Greeny's probably right, we won't find him for years and years". "Perhaps he sleeps near the witches cave", suggested Bluey. "I doubt it", Orangey said, "she would have probably woken him up to question him about all the cruel happenings in the past, when they tortured people and put them in dungeons and kept them prisoners for years and years.

Goldie, who had been rather quiet, suddenly joined in the conversation, "I think the best place to try is down by the waterfall. It is the place where we first met him". "Of course that was during the day", added Orangey, "but you could be on the right track. We'll start looking there straight away". "There may be a cave under the waterfall", suggested Cyani taking hold of Bluey's hand, "Can we go in pairs again?". "I think we had better all stay together", replied Orangey.

So they hurried along the green river bank with its drooping weeping willows nearly dipping into the water, until they reached the waterfall with its white foam splashing in all directions. "Careful not to get your wings wet", they reminded one another. "Cripes", shouted Bluey, "It's beginning to rain harder, now we're in for it".

They clustered together under the shelter of the massive oak trees, and looked up at the cold grey rock of the waterfall. "It's no use", remarked Caramilla, "we're getting wetter and wetter", as the water dripped from the trees onto them, and began to run down their necks. Bluey chipped in, "We soon won't be able to fly. We'll have to find a niche in the rocks where we can get some real shelter".

"Look, here's a spot", shouted Bluey. "Well, let's all get in then", responded Pinky. "There's not much room though", Greeny observed. "It's great fun though", retorted Bluey pressing close to his fairy friend, Cyani. "Watch out or you'll break my wand", she giggled, wriggling closer to him.

"Oh dear", exclaimed Caramilla, "I do believe it's getting wetter by the minute. Why don't we use our magic to help find the wretched ghost quickly?". "OK", agreed Orangey, "We'll do it together".

So all eleven fairies raised their wands, and with Orangey and Goldie standing in the centre controlling the magic action; they waited expectantly for the result. They witnessed that in no time at all they had created a combined audio and visual beam, which vibrated with great power, onto the rocks above them.

After only a few seconds they heard a strange sound, growing louder and louder. Suddenly a faint outline was pictured on the rock face right at the top of the waterfall.

It improved into the shadow of a man wearing a drab cloak, a hood partially covering his features. "Look, it's him. I'm sure it's him!", Orangey cried out.

The sound waves increased in volume, until they were becoming deafening. "It sounds like a giant snoring", said Bluey. Then eventually the picture intensified and the ghost could be seen clearly, crouching in a small cave to the right of the highest rocks. Feeling very elated, they concentrated the beam onto one spot. Then the opening in the cave lit up with a hazy light, and a large shape floated to the ground right in front of them making the smaller fairies gasp with fright. As they gazed with fascinated eyes, the shape slowly materialised into the solid body of the ghost.

He uncovered his face, and stood to his full height, tall and powerful, and then he spoke in his soothing melodic tones, but with a trace of annoyance. "What is it that you want of me?" he demanded. "I've found your house", shouted Orangey raising his voice above the sounds of the splattering downpour. The ghost's face changed, his sunken eyes became piercingly blue, his tight mouth swelled into a smile, and the contours of his face filled out, until a lithe handsome man stood there facing them. He held out his hand to Orangey, "Please, take me there immediately, I've very little time left", he pleaded.

As he and Orangey made to leave, he waved goodbye, and smiled at them all lighting up the night with the brilliant glow from his eyes. This time there was no mistake, Orangey was certain of the way, and in only a few moments of time, they arrived outside a magnificent

Tudor mansion. The huge oak door studded with iron rivets stood between them and the end of their search. Unhesitatingly the ghost placed one of his massive black keys into the lock, and the door swung open without a sound. He was well and truly home at last.

The ghost entered through the portal with Orangey close behind. They found themselves in a long hall with a solid shining wood floor. Hanging from the walls was an array of medieval weapons, pistols, swords, lances, heavy iron maces with savage looking chains attached. At the far end of the hall hung family portraits, and between the largest paintings was one of a man with blue eyes, and another of a striking woman dressed in a crimson gown. The man was holding a shining sword with a beautiful jewelled handle, and written underneath the words 'Pierehurst House in the year of our Lord 1563'.

The ghost could not contain himself any longer; he rushed to the end of the hall and grabbed the sword from the wall. He dashed up the huge stairway brandishing it, rushed in and out of the rooms to check, unlocking and then locking the doors. However it seemed to make him very happy.

Suddenly the ghost appeared to calm down and floated silently past Orangey, and stopped at a particularly huge oak door halfway along the main hallway. He unlocked it and disappeared again.

Orangey shrugged, "I suppose that's what ghosts are good at", he thought. "I expect it leads to the dungeons. I wonder what he wants from there?" In only a few seconds the ghost reappeared with a tall dusty bottle of wine. He poured it into two pewter goblets, and held one out for Orangey to drink. They shared the wine together in a toast to celebrate the achievement, although Orangey was too polite to say he didn't enjoy the taste one little bit.

The ghost beckoned and they ascended the broad staircase to the gallery above. The ghost unlocked yet another door and they climbed higher, and then onto a spiral staircase that led them out onto the roof. The ghost stood leaning against the turrets, obviously exhausted from his exertions, and gazed out across the view of the quiet green fields. They could see for miles along the river, right out over the two small woods on either side of the building.

The ghost murmured, "It's not exactly the same view that I enjoyed hundreds of years ago, but it is my house, my family's house, and I shall protect it for ever". He held out his hand to Orangey, holding his with a firm grip, they shook hands, smiling at each other. Then the ghost turned to the centre of the great house and spoke in a commanding voice, "On behalf of the founder of this family, and the generations since, we thank you".

Orangey never saw the ghost again, but a few weeks later, Orangey's father kept his promise and took the boys to visit the historic house. As they entered through the massive doorway, Orangey could feel the presence of the ghost, and was positive he was happy and content at last. He even had the idea that the portrait in the main hall which looked most like Piere the ghost, winked at him.

ORANGEY AND THE
CHRISTMAS DONKEY

Orangey and his brothers, Bluey, Greeny and Pinky, were playing happily in the snow, enjoying the exceptional cold weather during the weeks leading up to Christmas.

In their parents' thatched cottage the open fire crackled with slow burning logs collected from the forest. The warm baking smells emitting from the kitchen soon reminded them of how hungry they always became when playing out in the cold.

Their Mother and Father tried to give them all that they could reasonably afford. In particular, their Mother provided plenty of freshly baked cakes, delicious assorted puddings, varied topped pizzas, although the usual favourite was the minted lamb hamburgers in home baked seeded buns.

This year however there was likely to be precious little money left over for extras, and certainly none for presents.

The brothers continued to play excitedly in the fallen snow, screaming with delight as hastily made snowballs found their mark. Later they collected the newly fallen snow forming it into a huge mound, ready to transform it into a monster snowman. In their happy-go-lucky play, they were completely unaware of their parents worries with regard to providing them with the traditionally expected Christmas presents.

Next morning bright and early, and before his brothers had even stirred, Orangey set off for the village alone. As he trudged through the snow it crunched under his heavy boots. He spotted the robin sitting on the icy hedge as it chirped, and fluttered off in search of food.

Near the end of the road, just as he reached the outskirts of the village, he saw a cart heavily laden with freshly hewn logs being pulled by an old grey skinny donkey. The ribs around his flank were sticking out, showing open sores on his coat. With his head held low, he breathed great gasping billows of steam into the icy air. A tall angular man with a weather-beaten swarthy complexion, and wearing an extremely dirty and tatty overcoat, was whipping the animal in an effort to make it go faster. The wretched donkey could hardly move the cart, and Orangey noticed flecks of blood mingled with the vapour pouring from its nostrils. As he drew closer he could see matted blood on the donkey's back and flanks. In horror he shouted out to the man to stop thrashing the animal. The man peered at Orangey through shaggy grey-black eyebrows, his red rimmed piggy eyes glinting. He sneered, "And what will you do if I don't stop, you little beggar?". He turned towards Orangey flourishing his whip threateningly, and added, "Now run along or I'll put the whip across your shoulders". Orangey was not in the least frightened, and the brute had no way of knowing that although Orangey looked like any other small boy, he and his brothers were in fact elves, and as most of you know, Orangey was a 'magic elf', endowed with unusual powers. Normally he would not use them when grown-ups were around as they would not understand what was happening, but on this occasion, he was so upset, he felt he just had to try and help the donkey.

Being so early in the morning there were no other passers-by, so Orangey took the opportunity to teach the fellow a lesson. He stared at the man, and then blinked his eyes, immediately the whip flew out of the man's hand and landed in the snow. In quick succession Orangey blinked twice more, and the cruel creature tumbled out of the cart and fell with a thump onto the frozen road. As he tried to rise a massive invisible weight pressed into his back and forced him face downwards into the icy snow.

"What's happening? I can't get up", he shouted in surprise. Only now did Orangey allow a slight smile to appear on his face. "I'll let you up if you unhitch the donkey from the cart and give him to me", he said, in a quiet firm voice. "What?" spluttered the man, "Give him to you for free? Not bleedin' likely". Orangey stood there looking down at the wretch. "You know he's far too old to be still working". The fellow made a move as if to try and get up. However the strange weight on his back seemed to have increased, pushing his face further down into the snow, and making him splutter again and cough hoarsely. He raised his head gingerly and looked at Orangey with a baffled expression on his face, reluctantly murmuring, "Alright son you can have him, but how will I be able to get the cart home without him?". "You look pretty big enough and strong enough to me". Orangey answered, "I suggest you unload half the load and push it home yourself". Grumbling under his breath, the man scrambled to his feet, and with trembling hands unhitched the donkey that stood there shaking with cold and fear. Uttering another grunt the fellow threw most of the logs into the ditch, and then with a furtive glance at Orangey, he slowly started to push the cart down the road away from the village. "And don't come back", shouted Orangey, "or it'll be the worse for you". Muttering and cursing the disgraced vagabond managed to trundle the cart further along the road. As he went he mumbled, "I just don't understand it, it's not as though I've been drinking". He slipped on the ice and nearly fell. However, using the cart as support he managed to remain upright. He took another sidelong glance at Orangey, possibly wondering if he could catch him by surprise and attack him. However, shaking his head in bewilderment, decided that he'd had enough, so he kept going until he was out of sight around the first bend in the road.

Orangey took hold of the donkey's bridle, and soothing it with soft words, gently led him back towards the cottage. The poor animal could only walk slowly, and was still puffing and blowing as though still pulling a heavy load.

When they reached the cottage, Orangey persuaded the frightened donkey to enter the garden, and tied it to the rear fence overlooking the forest. He then hurried into the garden shed and mixed together some corn and hay his father kept for the chickens. Placing a substantial quantity into a bucket, and hoping that it was the correct feed, he offered it to the donkey, who stood there just looking at it not believing his good fortune. "Come on lad, eat up", Orangey cajoled. "You won't get better without eating". With this encouragement the donkey bent down stiffly and began to munch.

Leaving him quietly savouring his food, Orangey entered the side door leading into the kitchen, and returned with a bowl of warm water and a sponge and soft brush. Then very gently he cleaned and bathed the donkey from head to hoof. Overcoming his apprehension the animal nuzzled into him, and then whinnied softly.

Later on Orangey told his parents that he had found the donkey wandering on its own. Which wasn't quite true, but being kind country folk they agreed that he could look after the donkey until it was well again.

Two weeks passed by, and the weather did not relent but remained freezing. The donkey now had a permanent home in the shed, and with Orangey's care and excellent grooming, plus the regular feeding, had put on weight. Even his coat was beginning to shine with his new found health. It seemed that in no time at all, the donkey was becoming a beautiful animal. He kicked up his heels, and neighed with pleasure whenever any of the boys approached him. "Cor", exclaimed Bluey, "I reckon we'll be able to ride him into the forest soon". "Yeah, I'll be... what's that cowboy's name, Glint Eastwood?" asked Greeny. "It's not Glint, it's Clint, and as you are always running out of pocket money, perhaps we should call you

Skint Eastwood!" "Oh very funny", Greeny sneered, "at least I spend my money, not always saving it like you. We'll have to call you Scrooge". He ducked hastily as Bluey aimed the hens' bowl at him. It sailed through the air, and then slowed down and hovered over the frozen ground before settling softly down in front of him. They both turned round in amazement to see Orangey standing there glaring at them. "Lucky I managed to prevent that bowl from crashing on the hard ground, or you'd have both been in trouble from Dad". Then he added harshly, "and no one rides that donkey until I say he's ready ... don't forget". The two brothers shuffled off mumbling under their breath something about someone being a spoilsport. "By the way", asked Pinky, "will we ever be able to ride him?"

I'm not sure", replied Orangey, "You know he's been very sick". "He'll get better though won't he?" inquired Bluey, "he looks a lot better already". "Well I hope so. I know he appears to be okay, but I don't know how strong he is yet". Orangey grabbed the donkey's halter and led him out of the shed so that they could have a good look at him. "See how white his muzzle is? He's certainly an extremely ancient animal and should probably have retired years ago". He felt his legs, "I think hauling heavy loads has taken a lot out of him, he's only good for retirement".

How do you know that?" asked Bluey.

Orangey hesitated before answering, "I think it's obvious, he's just worn out".

However, secretly while his parents were in bed, and without even his brothers being aware, Orangey had been taking him into the forest at night as a special treat. He had also introduced him to the fairy sisters, who were delighted with him. They had taken turns riding him around the magic circle, each wanting to be next. As they were light and dainty he was strong enough to have carried them all together, but he found it more fun to have the pretty fairies in their gorgeous differently coloured dresses ride him one by one. Competitively, each one wanting him to go faster than the last, and soon finding a way of tickling him with their wands on either ear, encouraging him to turn and gallop at full stretch.

Within a few nights by, either tickling his ears or tapping him gently on the neck with their wands, they could change direction, and were soon making sweeps of wider and wider circles. Finally zigzagging through the wood in all directions, often ending up with a wild canter right back into the centre of the magic circle.

Fairy Cyani, returned from one such exploit, wiping her streaming eyes, and crying out, "Did you see the speed we reached that time? You know I think he's much faster than the old witch Haggotty on her broomstick". "Well I'm not sure about that", replied the fairy's leader, Caramilla, "but he's so nice he can be my white charger any day".

"What's that"? cackled a throaty voice, and from behind one of the tall elm trees sidled the witch herself. And of course dragging drearily behind her, was Spooks her slightly potty cat. She seemed decidedly pleased with herself. "What's happened to your usual lookout, the old owl? He certainly didn't see us arrive this time did he?". She cackled with glee, and bent down to pat Spooks. As she stood up they gasped to see that she was holding a great rawhide whip in her hand. She cracked it sharply in the direction of the donkey, and rasped, "This will make him go faster like nothing else I know".

"You really are a wicked old wanton", cried Cyani bursting into tears, "Why don't you go away and mind your own business!". "Now that's not a very nice thing to say", grated the witch, "I heard you saying that your donkey, as ugly as he is, could run faster than my broomstick". She carelessly smoothed Spooks fur the wrong way, making it stick up in clumps, before the riled cat could hiss in fury she grinned showing her yellow stumps, and spat "I have an idea, let's have a race, and the winner gets the donkey".

"Hold on", interrupted Orangey, who was sitting quietly on a moss covered log close by. "He's already our donkey. What do we get if we win?".

"Well although it's most unlikely, if you win I'll get you and your brothers the best Christmas presents you have ever set eyes on".

"Well I suppose so", as with some trepidation Orangey agreed that there would be a race the following night, and after midnight when the moon was at its brightest. Spooks let out a squeak of delight as it was agreed that the course to be covered, included running right through the centre of the forest, around the waterfall, and back via the witch's cave. "Why do you think Spooks was so happy when it was agreed to run down by the witch's cave?" queried Caramilla.

"No doubt he has some plan to upset us even more", wailed Cyani starting to cry again.

"Don't worry", mused Orangey, "we just might have a plan of our own", he patted the donkey who neighed softly in response.

The following night as the moon broke slowly through the grey clouds, it shone its pale silvery beams on a scene of great excitement. Haggotty the witch had arrived in a frantic whirl sitting complacently on a brand new broomstick. The brothers and fairies were fascinated to spy Spooks dressed in jockey's silks of black and purple, sitting behind and grinning manically.

Without further ado, the starting flag was raised and then dropped to start the contest. Haggotty shot off in a flash, her broomstick leaving behind it a shower of red and yellow sparks. As the witch disappeared into the trees, the donkey ridden by the dainty Cyani trotted around the huge oak tree, and then stood on the winning line calmly munching the grass.

Barely two minutes later the witch came screaming round the old oak and up to the winning line of holly berries shining crimson against the shadow of the dark trees. Her mouth fell open as she realised that the donkey was already there unconcernedly cropping the shoots of grass poking through the covering snow.

As she came to a halt, Spooks fell off the end of the broomstick and padded up to the donkey with his tail straight up in the air. "It's not possible", hissed Haggotty, "No one can go faster than me". The donkey neighed suddenly right in the face of Spooks, who back-pedalled quickly, then arched his back, and showed his sharp yellow teeth in a horrible grimace. "Well you must be wrong", Caramilla spoke softly to Haggotty. "When will you be bringing the presents?" she added with a smile. "Bah" spat the witch, "we'll see about that". She got astride the broomstick and as Spooks clambered on behind, she leered at them, and chanted "Fairies who cheat, and donkey's who fly, I'll make sure that someone will die". Her broomstick floated off slowly, and they could hear Haggotty's evil cackle, as she circled overhead and then set off for her cave to brew a spell in her own good time. The group of fairies and brothers looked up at each other in despair. "I don't think that was a very good idea", Bluey whispered.

"It was the only way of getting rid of her, she would have only thought of some other ruse to frighten you all", replied Orangey, and swung on his heel leading the donkey towards home.

He turned briefly as he walked, and waved the fairies goodbye, they smiled hesitatingly and fluttered into the magic circle, the brothers trailed unhappily after Orangey and the donkey. Caramilla appeared most unhappy, and asked her fairy sisters if they had any ideas that might help guard against the witch's threats. They shook their heads in unison. They discussed the problem well into the early morning, but failed to find a satisfactory solution. "What did she mean that someone will die?" asked fairy number five, Evangeline. "I'm afraid that we will have to wait and find out", answered Caramilla. They held hands and shivered with fear, as the sun glinted early red and yellow rays over the trees. "The red and yellow of the sun's rays remind me of the sparks flying out from the witch's broomstick", whispered Cyani. They shuddered and flew off into the forest to hide.

That year the village Christmas Festival had been arranged for the weekend before Christmas Day. A carol singing evening, and a tableau depicting Joseph and Mary with the baby Jesus in a manger had been planned. It was hoped to bring an assortment of farmyard and domestic animals to complete the scene. There were as always plenty of volunteers ready to play the main characters, but there was some difficulty in finding suitable animals. At the village meeting it was finally agreed that the Doctor's goat would be acceptable as he could be hobbled to stop him eating everything in sight. An especially docile black and white cow was offered by a local farmer, but. there was a doubt about the suitability or availability of any others. After some prompting from Orangey, his father suggested to the committee that they might consider the donkey. After seeing what an even-tempered beast it was, the donkey was selected to be part of the tableau and to lead the religious procession through the town to the Church.

On Christmas Eve, which was the Saturday prior to Christmas Day, a fresh layer of snow fell lightly covering the roads and pathways. That evening with a bright moon outlining the bare branches of the trees, highlighting the glistening frost and the covering snow made a beautiful setting for the tableau.

It was generally agreed that except for the extreme cold, the decision to organise a procession through the village with the ancient donkey leading, was a good one. The villagers were delighted at how disciplined the donkey behaved. His important role was to stand by the manger and look at the baby Jesus. This he did while swishing his tail happily.

Of course, he looked a completely different animal to the one who had been so badly treated. The several weeks of good food and grooming, had filled out his spare frame. Even his sores had healed, and his coat was now silky and gleaming, thanks to the brothers' turns at grooming him. The donkey was beside himself with pleasure, as it was the first time for years that he had not had to work hard pulling a heavy loaded wagon. He realised he was now treated and fed well, and since his coat had grown over the bare patches, he felt and looked quite handsome.

He sighed to himself with happiness, and thought that not many donkeys had been chosen for such an important part in a religious tableau, or indeed to lead the procession. He shuddered slightly as it came to him that he might have still been living with his previous owner and having to suffer the beatings and carrying terrible loads, he shuddered again.

That night after the celebrations were finished, he was taken home and given an extra tasty feed of malt biscuits with crunchy cornflakes, and then slept on a pile of sweet smelling hay.

In the bedroom that same night the boys were chattering excitedly about the presents they hoped to receive the following day. There was great fun ferreting around for clean socks, before they finally hung them up at the end of their beds in youthful expectation.

Little did they know, that at that very minute their parents were sitting in front of the dying fire, sadly discussing how best to tell the boys that there would he no presents for them this Christmas.

They tried to console each other with the knowledge that they were providing a super Christmas tree from the forest, with decorations of holly with bright red berries, and sprigs of green and white mistletoe hanging from the beams. In addition money had been saved for a traditional Christmas feast of turkey with chestnut and herb stuffing, roast potatoes, fresh vegetables from the garden, to be followed by homemade Christmas plum pudding and flaky pastry mince pies with clotted cream. Even so they went to bed with heavy hearts, reluctant to break the news to the boys until the last possible moment.

Later that night the shed door swung open, and the donkey poked his head out and sniffed the cold night air. Snow was falling again, as he trotted carefully off into the forest.

The way was lit by the bright moonlight that shone like a beacon, reflecting off the snow-laden branches. Fairly quickly he reached the fairie's magic circle, and neighed softly. There was no response, so he neighed a little louder. Within a few seconds tiny lights appeared flitting out of the surrounding trees, and rapidly eleven gorgeous fairies were gathered around him in anxious expectation.

"What do you want?" they asked in breathless unison. "Fancy coming into the forest alone at night?".

"Well you see", explained the donkey, "I have a problem that I hope you will help me with". He then explained that just a few days previously he had overhead the boys' parents talking in the garden, saying that they did not have sufficient money to buy presents for the four brothers this year.

"Oh dear", cried Cyani, "Of course we'll help won't we?" she turned her tearful face to the others. In chorus they asked, "What do you want us to do?". The donkey then outlined his plan. "Can you muster the forest animals, the happy gnome and his friends, and any others that can help as well", he suggested. "Of course we will", the fairy sisters spoke together.

So that Christmas Eve hasty preparations were made. Honey was collected from the bees' secret hoard and placed into earthenware pots, bags of nuts were offered by the squirrels from their precious hiding places, and everyone else in the woods joined in doing what they did best. The happy gnome and his friends constructed four coloured wooden sledges, the rabbits spun scarves made from their own wool, a hat with a feather or two was produced by the birds, and the baby badger handed over his week's pocket money. One of the old stags who lived deep in the wood, offered his last year's antlers to hang in the brothers' father's study, where he kept his old books. Although they all worked with gusto through the night, it was necessary for Caramilla to add a final touch by waving her wand over the gifts, and producing a host of varying toys that children adore.

Just before dawn the donkey walked slowly down the track back to the cottage, laden with two sacks of presents. On the way home the beavers from the river stopped him to add their gifts of Davy Crockett type fur hats, and a crowd of baby rabbits came bobbing up the path clutching fur mittens to add to the special load. Laden as he was, the donkey thanked everyone many times for all their help, and finally reached the cottage.

On Christmas morning, Orangey as usual, was up early to give the donkey his breakfast, and to his surprise saw him standing by the front door laden down with an amazing assortment of parcels. The fairies had even managed to pack most of them in brightly coloured wrapping paper, and had then sprinkled them with fairy dust so that they twinkled even in the dark.

"Cripes", cried Orangey. "Wherever did you get all these super packages from?". I hope they were not too heavy for you". The donkey shook his head and neighed out loud, "Nothing to the loads I've had to carry", he insisted. "Shush! You'll wake everyone up", cautioned Orangey. So without another sound, most of the parcels, and packages plus some unwrapped presents were carefully unloaded and placed under the Christmas tree. Orangey guessed that the antlers were for his Father's study, so he put them to one side. Hearing movement from upstairs, Orangey hurriedly took the remainder of the parcels and gifts and hid them in the donkey's shed out of sight. He was just in time as the boys' footsteps thundered down the stairs, and they arrived carrying their empty stockings. Pushing past Orangey, they spied the mass of presents stacked under the tree. Shouting with glee they began to sort them according to name and desire.

With all the din and excitement the scene was completed when Mr and Mrs Rangey appeared to find out what all the noise was about. They were dumbstruck to see the room filled with toys and parcels galore. They became even more surprised to find that they had presents too. "How on earth did this happen?" they asked no one in particular incredulously. "I really don't know", said Orangey keeping his fingers crossed behind him. "You see, when I came downstairs this morning, the old donkey was standing outside loaded up to the eyeballs. You'll have to ask him. But of course he can't talk", he added craftily.

When the Christmas dinner was finally finished, and all the mess had been cleared away, Orangey suddenly "discovered" the other presents in the shed. "This is unbelievable", cried their parents, "Whoever could this unknown Father Christmas be?". With so many extra gifts it was decided to load up the donkey, and take them to the Children's Hospital which was situated on the far side of the village. It was a long two and a half mile walk, and the donkey was pleased to reach the gates. "Still not as bad as hauling a great heavy cart through the snow for miles", he consoled himself.

As they reached the hospital grounds he could see some of the children crowding round the windows waving to him. Their smiling faces gazing at him in expectant pleasure. His heart swelled with pride, and although he was tired, he stood with his head held high, thoroughly delighted to feel so useful again.

While the gifts were being distributed among the sick children, two nurses came out to him and gave him a pat; one kissed his nose, and said "Now that's what I call a real Christmas Donkey"! "He must have been sent by Santa", suggested the other one.

By the time they returned home it was dark, so the donkey was given his supper and a special goodnight kiss, and placed in his shed for the night. When everyone in the cottage had at last gone to bed and it was still and quiet, the donkey pushed open the shed door, and looked up at the sky. It was a gloomy eerie night with the light from the moon only showing from time to time. Large flakes of snow settled briefly on his nose and ears, he uttered a little sad sigh, shuddered in the frosty cold, and then set out for the forest.

After his exertions during the past two days, he felt terribly tired, and walked slowly. However he knew exactly where he was heading, so without hesitation he bypassed the fairies' magic circle, and hobbled further into the depths of the wood. About two hundred yards or so further on, he staggered slightly, then knelt down and rolled over. His eyes alighted on the tall oaks, and then the smaller upright green pines. He noticed the mossy banks beneath had escaped from the fall of snow. As he closed his eyes for the last time, he heard scurrying creatures nearby. He was pleased that this spot would be his home forever, and he would always be near his friends. It was just as well he did not see Haggotty the witch zoom by on her broomstick, her black clothed body outlined against the waning moon. She cackled and waved her fist, then shot off towards her cave, with Spooks clinging on behind in a desperate attempt to keep his balance.

The following morning Orangey became rather anxious as he opened the shed door, as there was no sign of the donkey. He then noticed the hoof prints in the snow, half hidden by a layer of hoar frost. He tracked the prints walking quickly. The trail took him past the magic circle and into the centre of the forest. He almost lost the trail, but luckily spied a new mound. It was already covered in twigs, with long grass and loosened moss scattered over it. The forest animals had already lovingly concealed their old friend.

Standing there alone in that solitary cold spot, and feeling so agonisingly sad, Orangey remembered that with the coming of spring, the mound would become a bower of wild flowers as a monument. This particular place in the forest would always be special he thought. But even so, bright, clear tears rolled down his cheeks, as he realised he would never see his Christmas donkey again.

ORANGEY GETS
A HISTORY LESSON

Orangey left the classroom with Miss Timson-Jones' words ringing in his ears. "Ossie Rangey your mind is full of frivolous things. You'll never learn history properly until you concentrate in class". He shook his head trying to get rid of her nagging voice. "She's just like the witch", he uttered aloud. He decided that with her long nose and thin mouth, and continual harping, she really reminded him of the witch Haggotty. Especially when the fearsome witch hissed with rage at the fairies.

Orangey had three brothers whose names you will remember are, Bluey, Greeny and Pinky. Although they looked like other small boys, they were really elves. It was only Orangey who was a 'magic elf', and possessed remarkable powers.

"Thank goodness", he mused as he set off for home, "tomorrow is Saturday; I'll play in the forest the whole weekend, and try and forget school and its problems".

The following day he walked alone alongside the sparkling river, until he reached the waterfall with its bubbling white water, and watched it cascading over the jagged rocks.

He sat down in the sun to collect his thoughts, and ponder about the games he and his brothers might play later in the day. He expected that his brothers were already playing one of their more boisterous games, somewhere in another part of the wood. "Probably pretending to be marauding pirates, or Robin Hood and his Merry Men", thought Orangey.

He lay there trying to relax, but anxiously thinking about his grandfather who only that morning had been taken into hospital. He knew that his parents were rather worried about his health, as he was becoming rather elderly, and lived alone.

Orangey squinted his eyes in the sun's strong rays, until opening them slightly he noticed an unusual tall tree that looked surprisingly bare of leaves considering that it was summer. Even more strangely, right at the top a flag was flapping in the light breeze. "How could there be a flag on top of a tree in the middle of the forest?" he wondered, and tried to doze off again.

Without warning a voice bellowed out, and then he imagined he could hear muffled curses, and a strong smell of salt water wafted to his nostrils. The voice rang out again, this time nearer, and he heard the words clearly, "Get aloft you lazy good-for-nothings". He opened his eyes fully, and was startled to see a swarthy man dressed in dungarees, with a soiled white shirt open to the waist.

More frighteningly, in his belt he wore a wicked looking dagger, a black patch over one eye, and a fearsome looking whip in his hand that snaked out and cracked loudly just above Orangey's head.

Without waiting for the whip to strike again, Orangey scrambled to his feet, and became aware of an unusual swaying movement below him. He glanced round and spied white-topped waves bearing down on him. However, they crashed against a wooden structure and only showered him with spray. Only then did he realise that somehow he was on the deck of an old fashioned sailing ship under full sail.

Completely baffled by his strange surroundings, and how he got there, he frantically leapt up into the ship's rigging, and started climbing up the mast hand-over-fist.

As he got higher, he saw other small boys scaling the masts on either side, and adjusting the ropes as they climbed. High above him was a wooden cradle, which later he was told was known as a crow's nest. In it stood an older boy looking out to sea through a long brass telescope. He seemed to be calling out numbers, and from time to time shouted them out to a muscular sailor standing on the lower deck.

He was a massive man, with huge muscles standing out prominently and rippling in the gleaming sunlight. He pulled easily on the ship's huge steering wheel, although the high wind swept most of his words away, Orangey could just make out him saying, "Aye aye bosun", to the sailor holding the whip still held firmly in his hand.

As Orangey neared the top of the mast, the ship plunged downwards into a green white flecked wave, and lurched suddenly on its side. He held on tightly, but above him he saw the older boy stumble and fall over the shallow rail of the crow's nest. The telescope went shooting out of his hand and landed onto the cradle floor. In a split second he came hurtling towards Orangey, and if he had struck into him, they would both surely have fallen to certain death onto the wooden deck.

Orangey blinked his eyes frantically, and an invisible force slowed the boy as he fell. Orangey thrust out his left hand and grabbed him by his collar, holding onto him tightly. The boy opened his eyes and clutched the mast with both hands, and stuttered, "Cor mate, I thought I was a goner then". Taking a deep breath, he slowly and carefully climbed back up the mast, and into the crow's nest, then looked anxiously ahead for any other following huge waves, and started shouting directions to the sailor below.

That evening after a hard day's work, Orangey sat with the older boy and three others in a smelly alcove in the ship's hold. It was dark and the smell quite awful. "You're a right 'ero, you were mate, holding out your 'ands and catching me like that". He scratched his ear and continued, "Come to think of it, I don't know 'ow you did it with all my weight, I'm twice as big as you are". He then looked accusingly at Orangey. "We 'avn't seen you before, and we're two days out of Plymouth, and bound for the Azores. Where 'ave you been 'iding? You're not a blinking stowaway are you?".

Orangey was still in shock, the events of the day had been

so traumatic, he couldn't understand how he'd got aboard ship, and where he really was. When he was told that the year was 1813, he nearly fainted. "That's two years before the battle of Waterloo", he said. "What's that you say?" demanded the older boy. "Um, no matter", mumbled Orangey looking away.

After five and a half uncomfortable hours clinging to the mast, the bosun had ordered him to get below, and with one eye on the whip, he had hastily climbed down a succession of rusty rings until he reached the hold.

The other boys had shown him the way to the galley on the climb down. After the older sailors had eaten the boys were given a hard tack biscuit, and a mug of hot gruel. He was so cold and hungry that he hardly noticed that the biscuit tasted rather like a smelly dog biscuit, and that the disgusting gruel had green bits floating on the top.

He suddenly felt terribly tired and asked "Where do we sleep?". The smallest boy with tousled ginger hair pointed to the floor. "There", he said, "and don't pinch my sacking". Just as Orangey settled down on the cold wooden planks he heard a rustling sound, and turned slightly, and found himself looking into the eyes of a huge black rat. It showed its sharp yellow teeth in a horrible grimace, and then ran under some dirty sacking. As Orangey paled with shock, the older boy laughed and said, "It's only a rat, nothing to worry about, there's plenty of them down 'ere. If they get really hungry, they'll soon let you know". He slapped his sides with mirth, and spoke again, "anyway, what's your blinking name? Mine's Pete, and this 'ere is Tom, Dick and 'Arry", he indicated the other younger scruffy lads. Orangey could hardly stifle a laugh himself, "Tom, Dick and Harry", he echoed. He'd read in his history books that they were probably the most popular everyday names given to ordinary folk in the 19th century. "Cripes", he thought to himself, "I'm in the lost olden times, how do I escape from them?".

"Well, what's so funny mate?" the older boy, Pete, asked. "Oh, nothing", replied Orangey, "anyway my name's ...", he hesitated not knowing whether to say Orangey or Ossie, his everyday name. He decided on Ossie. "Er, Ossie Rangey", he replied eventually. "Oh your name's Rangey, your dad a farmer or something?". "Er kind of", he swallowed thinking about his home, his brothers, and mother and father. What would they be thinking, when he didn't come home for tea. How about if he didn't return for a month, or even a year. He shuddered and curled up on the floor to sleep, without saying another word.

In the morning, he woke suddenly to find the sun streaming through the hatch, and onto his pale face. As he moved he felt stiff and cold, and the sea air had given him an appetite. "Time to move", growled Pete, the obvious leader of the boys, and gave Orangey a nudge in the side. "It's almost five bells, the Captain will be inspecting the crew up on the deck in about half an hour".

They splashed their faces nearly clean, in a blackened water butt, filled with impure sea-water. On their trudge up to the deck, they each grabbed a hard biscuit and a mug of hot grog from the galley.

The grog made Orangey cough and splutter, "What's in

it?" he asked Pete. "Only a splash of dark rum, to keep out the morning mist", mumbled Pete. "Don't you like it?" Orangey hesitated. "E're give it to me", said Pete, knocking it hack in one gulp. He wiped his mouth with the back of his hand, "Not bad", he grinned, "something to cheer us up before we meet the Captain".

As they scrambled on to the deck, there was a great deal of activity. Sailors with buckets of sea-water were scrubbing the wooden deck, ropes were being curled and placed under bales of canvas in an attempt to tidy the ship.

What a motley assortment of humanity, thought Orangey, as he viewed them in their scruffy dungarees, sweat stained singlets and rope soled sandals, some with great gaping holes. The only concession to gaiety was an exceptional variety in the coloured bandeau holding back greasy unkempt hair. Many more drifted up from below into ragged lines, muttering between themselves as they waited impatiently for the Captain.

Orangey heard a deal of shouting and swearing from the poop deck, and a solitary sailor was dragged out onto the deck and tied to the mast. "What's happening ?" asked Orangey. "He's going to be punished by flogging", replied Pete, with a grin of expectancy on his face. "Flogging?" queried Orangey. "Yes, he'll probably receive fifty lashes, as 'e was found stealing food from the galley. Mind you, as it's 'is second time, if the Captain's in a bad humour, he might be 'ung", he added hopefully. "Shut up you scum", bellowed the bosun, and cracked his whip loudly, "unless you want a taste of the lash".

Orangey stared up at the poop deck, and saw a short squat

man, dressed in a dark blue uniform with a gleaming sword and scabbard buckled around his waist. There were several lines of silk braid on his shoulders, his three cornered hat partially covered his eyes, but they and his white teeth glistened against the black of his beard as he spoke.

His voice rang out across the ship, and a good portion of the crew cowered, and looked up at him through squinty eyes. "They all look guilty to me", thought Orangey, "I wouldn't trust any of them in a hurry".

The Captain's words were clear and precise. "You men have heard that this scum here", he pointed his sword at the wretch tied to the mast, "has been found guilty of stealing food, on evidence given by the bosun, the punishment for which is fifty lashes, and as this is a second offence, he'll be hung from the yard-arm at dawn tomorrow".

The ship's company growled, Orangey did not know whether in agreement or not, but the Captain continued talking. He looked sternly at the figure tied to the mast, "Are you ready for your punishment?" he barked. The man lifted his head, and Orangey saw that there was something familiar about his looks. His voice replied clearly and defiantly, "Captain you have listened to lies again, you have allowed your better judgment to be clouded by another's hate", he spat on the deck in the direction of the bosun.

Without a moments hesitation the Captain roared, "Start the punishment bosun". The bosun reached out and ripped the shirt from the man's back. Orangey could see ripples of raised angry looking flesh, from previous floggings.

The bosun motioned to the heavily built sailor wielding the whip, "Get your weight into it, and make every stroke count", he ordered. The lash whistled through the air and cut into the victim's back, leaving a new welt oozing blood from the first stroke.

Orangey could bear it no longer, and with one agile bound leapt onto the poop deck. The bosun and the sailor were amazed to see him appear by their sides so suddenly, and were not sure where he had come from. "Get away boy", snarled the bosun, "or you'll have some of the same". Orangey stood up to his full height, but still looked woefully small. "Put the whip down", he ordered the sailor in a quiet firm voice. The sailor looked at the bosun, who nodded angrily. He raised the whip to strike again, ignoring Orangey's command.

Orangey blinked swiftly and the whip flashed through the air, but this time instead of hitting the prisoner, it shot out of the sailor's hand and fell to the deck. Quickly the burly sailor bent and picked it up, and raised it again. Orangey blinked twice this time, and the whip flew out of the sailor's fist, and shot over the side and splashed into the sea.

The Captain roared with rage at the bosun and said, "Throw that little blighter into the sea to get it back". As the bosun stooped to pick Orangey up, he blinked yet again; this time the bosun reeled back as though struck by a thunderbolt, his rear hit the ship's rail and he was catapulted into the depths below. There was a loud shriek, followed by an even louder splash, and a lot of unpleasant garbled words, whose meaning were clear but unintelligible to the human ear.

Cheers suddenly broke out from the lines of men on deck, while the Captain and his officers drew their swords anticipating a possible mutiny, but none of the sailors took a step towards the poop deck.

"You", shouted the Captain, speaking to the sailor who had been wielding the whip, "grab that little whipper-snapper, and bring him up here".

Orangey was not sure what to do. He could hurl the sailor overboard with his magic powers, but decided that it was a good opportunity to speak to the Captain face to face, so he allowed the sailor to pick him up, which after a moment's thought, he hesitatingly did, and dumped Orangey in front of the Captain.

"Name", barked the Captain. Orangey did not reply. "I could have you flogged, or hung from the yardarm for assaulting a warrant officer, marooned on a desert island, clapped in irons, walk the plank", he paused for breath as his face turned puce.

There was a muted cheer from the assembled crew as the bosun's dripping head appeared above the ship's rail, followed by his soaking body. He stood there wet and cold with his clothes wrapped tightly around him.

"What sort of discipline do you call this bosun?" thundered the Captain. "Couldn't be 'elped Captain, 'e's a bloody stowaway", he whined, and looked threateningly at Orangey.

The Captain swung round on one heel to face Orangey. "Are you a stowaway boy?" he raged. "I don't think so", replied Orangey quietly. "Don't think so? We'll soon make you think", the Captain turned to his officers behind him. "Midshipman Conners", he ordered, "tie him up and dump him in the hold until I'm ready to deal with him".

A young lad not much older than Orangey, drew up to attention and saluted the Captain, "Yes sir, immediately", and then proceeded to walk towards Orangey. He was dressed in a smart uniform, with just a single strand of braid on his shoulders, but his three cornered hat teetered and slipped down over his ears.

"Quick about it", bellowed the Captain, galvanising the young officer into action. Orangey blinked his eyes and the midshipman stood rooted to the spot. Only his eyes were able to move, and they fixed on Orangey in a frightened stare.

The Captain was becoming rather agitated and unsure of himself, with the increasing pattern of events. In a sudden fit of panic, he decided to end the uncertainly once and for all, and drew his sword ready to strike Orangey down.

Then a perplexed gasp went up from the assembled crew, as the sword flew out of his hand and struck point down in the deck, quivering with the impact.

Desperately the Captain grabbed the hilt and tried to pull

it from the deck. He couldn't budge it, and then he found that he couldn't remove his hand from the hilt either.

Breathing heavily, he ordered his officers to attack Orangey, and slay him where he stood. Orangey blinked five times in quick succession, and the officers who had hardly moved, remained rigid, like so many blue china statues.

Rooted to the spot with the Captain still holding his trapped sword, he and his officers tilted first one way, and then the other, as the ship veered off course.

The crew on the deck below shuffled forward, and cheered and guffawed, and appeared ready to rush the Captain's bridge position. Realising this, he swivelled his eyes and looked directly at Orangey. In a quiet beaten voice whispered, "Alright my fellow, I don't understand what's happening, or who or what you are, but as the ship is in danger of floundering, I'll accept your command". As Orangey hesitated for a moment the Captain added, "If you release us, you have my word as an officer and a gentleman".

Orangey blinked his eyes and waved his hands in the direction of the Captain and his officers, the rigid figures softened and within a few seconds returned to full movement.

The Captain withdrew his sword from the deck and placed it in the scabbard. Drawing up to his diminutive but formidable full height, he barked his orders to the first mate, "Mr Teal, assume command and resume course".

Motioning to Orangey he said, "Come boy, follow me to my cabin. I must enquire more about you".

They went below deck, and as they entered the Captain's cabin, Orangey saw that it was quite large, with a solid oak desk in one corner, a brown leather chair, with crossed cutlasses decorating the wall beside a porthole. It was so different from the rest of the ship. It had its own elegance in a military manner, and the stink was so less noticeable, they could have been on another vessel.

The Captain slumped into his chair, and poured out a large tumbler of brandy and sunk it in one gulp. Then poured another immediately, and slurped it down. He pivoted in his seat and looked Orangey straight in the eyes. "Well boy are you God or beast?" he said softly. "Neither", replied Orangey, "I'm a person from a different time span, but endowed with strange and magical powers". The Captain looked a trifle alarmed and seemed to shrink in his massive leather chair. Orangey continued speaking in a low firm voice, "I believe in fairness and truth, perhaps I was sent here to warn you that one day in the future there'll be freedom and equality for all men and women". "An interesting notion", replied the Captain, "we could discuss it for a long time. However you do appear to have knowledge and power beyond the normal", he shrugged, "so I must accept your reasoning".

He got up from the desk, and paced up and down, "I've promised you command of this ship, and this is what you shall have". He paused, "but I feel there is something else you require of me". Orangey looked at the Captain squarely, "You are correct; there is one other thing I should like you to do, which is also important". Before he could continue the Captain held up his hand, and walked over to the porthole.

Underneath was a solidly built brass bound chest, he opened it, and took out a small blue uniform, with a matching three cornered hat. "Put them on", he ordered, "at least you'll look the part, these were for my young son, who I hoped would wear them one day".

Orangey felt honoured, and as he dressed, he resumed talking, "I'll be happy to sail the ship under your instructions, but firstly I must have your word on my second request". The Captain smiled, "Please ask me, I'm sure I'll be able to agree", he waited for the reply.

"The prisoner who is to be flogged and then hanged, what will become of him when I leave?". "Justice will be done", replied the Captain grimly, "the sentence must be carried out".

"Well I ask that you pardon him, I believe that you have been deceived in the evidence given to you". "I had an idea that you may ask me so", said the Captain, "there is some likeness in the two of you". "That's true" Orangey agreed, there is something familiar about his face to me. Is it possible you can let me know his name?". The Captain kicked open the cabin door, and bellowed for the bosun, a damp and bedraggled figure appeared in the doorway. "Find me the name of the culprit", he looked sideways at Orangey, and quickly added, "the unfortunate man, who it seems has a guardian angel".

The bosun opened the huge log, and thumbed down the

pages, he stopped at an entry written in bright purple ink. "Here is the name", he mumbled, "Oswald Rangey, aged twenty-four, a pressed man on his first voyage".

Orangey swallowed hard, he couldn't believe his ears, it seemed that he may save his great, great, great grandfather from hanging; mind you he was not sure how many greats the generations demanded. He now realised that the man looked like his own grandfather when he was younger. He remembered the pictures his father had shown him taken at his wedding some sixty years before.

The Captain led the way out onto the poop deck, and spoke to the still assembled crew. "I have reconsidered the verdict, the prisoner is to be released, allowed a day off duties, and given a double ration of rum for a week."

The front row of the crew shambled forward and one tall man with a bushy red beard cried out, "Good on you Captain, we knew you'd find out, that it was the blasted bosun that's been stealing".

The Captain had a strange understanding smile on his face, as he turned to Orangey and saluted, "You do have some interesting powers my boy, take over my ship I know it's in good hands".

For the next hour Orangey enjoyed himself giving the commands that sent the huge ship ploughing through the waves, ever further from the shores of England. Of course the Captain quietly instructed him in what to do, but it was still great fun for Orangey.

As the sun reached its highest point in the sky and beat

down on the ship, a sudden sea mist blew in over the deck. The prisoner who had been released by the Captain had been watching him carefully, and waved out as he caught Orangey's eye. The mist suddenly obliterated the mast, and then it appeared again in the bright sunlight, but this time it looked more like a tree, a figure strode out from under it, and said, "Wherever have you been, you've missed tea, and everyone wants to know where you are".

Orangey opened his eyes wide to find Bluey standing over him, "Come on", he said, "you look all bleary eyed. How long have you been asleep, and what's all that mumbling about a ship, a Captain, and that there's to be no hanging?". Bluey bent down to help him up, "Who's going to be hanged?" he asked. "I'm not sure now", replied Orangey sleepily, "but he did look a bit like granddad, and he had the same name". "Who did?" asked Bluey. "I promise to tell you some other time, but let's go home, I'm hungry", said Orangey.

ORANGEY MEETS
THE SEA MONSTERS

O rangey and his brothers Bluey, Greeny and Pinky were very excited as the very next day they were going off on holiday to the seaside. As they all lived together in an old thatched cottage on the edge of a pretty country village, bordered by green fields and a huge dark forest, a visit to the coast for the first time would be quite an experience for them.

That night after their parents were fast asleep, Orangey and his brothers flew out of the bedroom window and sped towards the centre of the forest. There they were to meet their friends the fairies, and tell them about the forthcoming trip to the seaside.

The boys looked like ordinary small boys to adults, but they were also elves, and Orangey was a 'magic elf' who had extraordinary powers which he used on their many adventures.

Pleased to be free, they flew through the wood. Firstly

they spotted the old barn owl, who often acted as their sentinel, but tonight he only blinked and hooted to them as they sped by.

Shortly after, they noticed a couple of gnomes hiding under an elm tree, who scuttled off just before the brothers reached the fairies' magic circle. Many of the gnomes in the forest were quite nasty, and tried to play rotten tricks on the fairies, and would even steal their wands if they thought they weren't looking.

The brothers, led by Orangey, descended right into the centre of the twinkling white lights. The fairies were waiting for them, however, their leader, Caramilla, was not her usual smiling self, and cried out, "We wish you had been here sooner, as you could have helped chase off two creepy gnomes who were lurking about here obviously up to no good". "Don't worry", replied Orangey, "they saw us coming and ran off further into the forest, you won't see them again tonight now that they know we are here".

The brothers then excitedly told the fairies about their forthcoming trip to the seaside, and added that they would be away for two weeks, and not to worry if they did not meet them for a while. The tiny fairies looked slightly crestfallen, "We've never been to the seaside either", they said, "but please be extremely careful, as we've heard from the seagulls that the sea can be terribly rough, and dangerous sometimes".

"We certainly will be careful", replied Orangey, "and you must be careful too, and keep a special lookout for the wicked witch, Haggotty". He looked around into the depths of the dark green forest and continued, "In fact, I'll ask the old barn owl to keep a special guard over you during the night. He can perch on a tall tree near you". "Mind you", said Caramilla, "the one good thing is, since Haggotty came to our party, and enjoyed herself so much, she hasn't worried us at all". "That's encouraging news of course", replied Orangey, "but if she's put into a temper by Spooks her crazy cat, or even by some other trivial matter, she may well become aggressive again". He thought for a moment, "I wonder if the gnomes have been spying on you, and telling her your whereabouts".

So after promising to be careful at all times, they waved goodbye to one another, with the brothers promising to bring back some unusual coloured shells for the fairies' garden.

Next day the boys dressed in their holiday clothes, and set off with their parents for Fishaven, a resort somewhere on the south coast. Late in the afternoon they reached a white and pink painted hotel, with a turreted tower on either side. The boys saw that the gardens, thick with shrubs and summer flowers, ran right down to the seashore; they wouldn't even have to cross a road.

For supper that night they enjoyed a real seafood treat. Starting with fresh shrimps, followed by poached halibut with white sauce, and lovely new potatoes covered with a garnish of parsley. The dessert consisted of sliced marinated oranges, with greengage blancmange, and pink strawberry ice-cream. "Every colour but mine", said Bluey. "Don't worry", they laughed, "the sea is blue, and there's plenty of that outside the window".

As it had been a long and tiring day travelling, they were packed off to bed early, and were delighted to find that they were sharing the same large room in the tower nearest to the sea. They could hear the waves crashing on the rocks, and from the window could see the frothy white foam running up the beach in rivulets, and nearly reaching the garden wall.

Later that night they climbed out of the window and flew quietly into the garden, and then walked the few yards to the beach. "Wow!", exclaimed Bluey, "Look at these beautiful shells, the fairies will love them". In the moon's pale light stretched hundreds of shapes of shells made up of many different colours. There were shells of crystal white, mottled blue, deep sea green, and pale pink. Some had curved edges, some scalloped, and just a few were diamond shaped with bright specks looking like tiny flecks of gold.

The boys slowly wandered off down the beach towards the rocks, voicing in wonder "Look at this one!", "Wow, no look at this super one!", "How about this one with the spiral top?".

They rambled on their voices becoming quieter as they moved further away looking for bigger and more spectacular shells, until they came to a rocky crag leading right out into the sea. It was covered with shiny-shelled cockles and winkles, firmly attached to the rocks, with fairly big waves breaking over the entire length of the rocks and showering them with spray.

"Remember what the fairies said", suggested Bluey, "At night that sea looks really grey and frightening. We'd better not go too far along the rock; it stretches right out to sea".

Orangey had stayed nearer to the hotel, looking for shells, but spotted tiny sand crabs waltzing by, then saw a dried starfish, and in a deep pool there were eels wriggling just under the water. He sat down on a rock and watched, fascinated at the moonbeams flitting about on the surface of the sea, before seeming to jump from rock to rock, finally to gleam brightly on the sea's surface.

By the light of one of the longer lasting beams he suddenly saw a huge silver fish that looked as though it was actually sitting on the rock next to his. As he stood up to get a closer view, it moved, and as the moonlight brightened again, he gasped with disbelief as sitting there combing her long silvery blonde hair was a beautiful mermaid. Behind her he could clearly see her tail, ending in a fish-like triangle.

She drew in her breath sharply as she saw him and looked ready to plunge into the sea. Before she could move Orangey whispered, "Don't go, you look so beautiful, I'd love to talk to you". She hesitated, thought for a moment and then shyly asked his name. "Orangey", he replied, and added, "I'm a magic elf". "An elf", she queried, "I've never met an elf before". "I've never met a mermaid", countered Orangey. "Do you live in the sea"? He looked out over the waves, "It looks so very cold and quite uninviting". She smiled and replied, "Yes, I live in the sea with my sisters and my father Neptune, he's away at present". Orangey was listening intently so she continued in her softly lilting voice, "It's not always so cold and scary. Once I swam all the way to Gibraltar, and sat on the biggest rock I've ever seen. I was so terribly tired, but it was worth it, as on the way I encountered an octopus with funny squiffy eyes, and long scaly arms with suckers on them. He wanted to give me a hug, but I decided to give him a miss". She flicked her silky hair from her eyes and continued with her story. "On the way back I just missed bumping into a great big stingray, who was swimming by in a hurry, and you should have seen the eels, huge black and silver ones, just like great big snakes". "Sounds jolly dangerous", said Orangey. "It can be", she replied, "but of course I'm used to it".

She moved slightly closer to him, "By the way", she asked, "can you swim?. I see you haven't got a tail". "I believe I could", muttered Orangey slightly taken aback, "but I've never tried". He shifted on the hard rock, "I can do most things", he added rather lamely.

Her eyes searched for his, shining as brightly as the stars overhead, "Perhaps you would like to come swimming with me", she lent forward silently, "I'll show you how, and I'll take you to a sunken wreck with a real treasure chest; it's a massive oak chest and I can't open it alone, but I think it's filled with golden coins, and precious jewels, and other valuable trinkets lost in a storm centuries ago".

Orangey couldn't believe his ears, he was being invited to go swimming with a beautiful mermaid, and search for sunken treasure. It all sounded too good to be true, what a super holiday this is going to be he thought. She moved to the edge of the rock, "Are you ready?", she asked. "I er think so", Orangey replied, "but I'm not sure if I can swim under water". To delay taking a final decision Orangey suddenly asked, "By the way, what is your name?". She smiled sweetly and sighed, "I'm Sylvie and my home is near here", and pointed to the rolling waves. "I'll tell you what, after locating the treasure, we'll go and meet my sisters".

"Yes, a good idea", said Orangey trying to find something to say to delay plunging into the cold green sea, "but I've got three brothers with me, and I must tell them first". Sylvie's face lit up with interest so he continued. "We live in an old house overlooking a wild forest, and living in it are fairies, and a wicked witch named Haggotty who lives in a cave with her slightly potty cat, Spooks". "Well it must be dangerous for you just walking in the wood", said Sylvie, "the witch could jump out and attack you at any time". "She'd have to be jolly quick", said Orangey rather smugly, "She hasn't managed it yet, anyway her silly cat is always falling off her broomstick if she goes too fast, and his squawking and meowing can be heard from miles away."

He stood up looking along the beach, "Right if I find my brothers and tell them where I'm going first, you can take me to the treasure", suggested Orangey. "Where are they now?" asked Sylvie. "They've gone over there near that rocky crag sticking out into the sea, I think", said Orangey peering into the gathering stormy darkness.

"Alright, I'll swim round and meet you by the edge of the rocks", said Sylvie. She dived into the sea, and all that was left were a few ripples on the surface of the grey green heaving waves.

Orangey felt strangely alone as he walked along the seashore calling out to his brothers. Once he thought he heard a reply, but it was only a seagull squawking overhead, then except for the swish of the sea it became eerily quiet. He reached some large rocks about four hundred yards from the crag, and in the distance he thought he could make out three tiny figures but they were completely still.

As he approached, to his horror, he saw that the still forms had been tied up with strands of slimy seaweed, with one plaited length trailing out into the sea. As he watched in the gloom he could just see three monster green crabs dragging the bodies down into the water. He shot into the air and flew rapidly along the shoreline. As he neared the scene, he realised that all three had been pulled right under the water and had already disappeared. Just before the cold dreadful sea closed over them, he saw the terrified looks on the faces of his brothers, as their eyes stared out from the strange shell helmets that had been forced over their heads.

Orangey was distraught; he'd arrived just seconds too late to save them. "What can I do now?", he said to himself, as he stood there helplessly watching the area of cold sea that had so recently closed over his brothers. Some bubbles rose to the surface, and Sylvie appeared paddling gently in the water.

"My brothers", gasped Orangey, "They've been dragged off by three great fearsome green crabs, at least five foot long", he appealed to Sylvie, "Do you think they are going to eat them?". "Well not straight away", replied Sylvie,

"You see it's the shark-men who train the crabs to catch unwary animals and small children who play by the water's edge". Her mouth turned down with distaste as she continued, "The giant crabs drag them into an underwater lair, and eventually they'll hand them over to the shark-men who'll eat anything that is caught. She added, "Mind you, there may be a delay as they will question them first to see if they can improve their technique of trapping young children, as they find them so deliciously tender", she shuddered.

"Shark-men", queried Orangey, "I've never heard of them". Sylvie sighed, "They're part men and part shark, made up of bits of both". Her eyes filled with tears as she told Orangey more about the wicked creatures. "They're horrible, but usually have men's heads with sharp pointed teeth, fins instead of arms, scaly tails in place of legs, mind you, I've seen some with a smaller tail, and one leg that they can hop on". She paused and added, "They are extremely dangerous because they can breathe under water, and can also survive on land for several minutes".

Orangey wailed with frustration, "I can't breathe under water, and my wings will get wet, and probably won't work anymore, and I'm not sure if my magic powers will function in the sea". "Now don't get yourself in a stew", soothed Sylvie, "I'll help you save them, but first we must get you a helmet so that you can breathe under water". Bending down gracefully she picked up a huge oval shell, and placed it over Orangey's head. She then flicked her fingers and spun a fine silver mesh around the sides until it fitted perfectly. Finally she produced even finer strands for the front section so that he could see through it.

Orangey breathed deeply, scraped his feet in the sand, and patted his clothes, instantly his orange tunic changed into a clinging waterproof oilskin suit. He now felt ready to take the plunge. "Follow me", shouted Sylvie as she dived deeply into the tormenting depths. Orangey took a rasping breath and followed immediately. Down they went; Sylvie held Orangey's hand and guided him past some jagged rocks, down even further, until it became gloomy and cold.

Orangey shivered, as a massive lobster with clutching claws grabbed at them, but Sylvie turned expertly and they glided by unhurt. Still holding Orangey's hand, she motioned to him, pressing her other hand to her lips in a sign to be quiet, and pointed directly ahead.

It was the mouth of an underwater cavern, with lights shining brightly in contrast to the dark green water. "Look out for electric eels", Sylvie whispered in his ear, "The shark-men use them to light the cave". She swam closer to him and whispered again, "Some of the largest ones can be used as weapons by sending shockwaves through the water, and a very big one could actually kill you if it touched you with its tail".

They swam carefully into the entrance where there were only small electric eels, being used as lights, and didn't seem to notice them as they floated by.

Sylvie flipped her tail vigorously and they shot rapidly upwards, and broke the surface of the water. They had emerged in a cave of solid rock, with a beach of fine white sand lying before them.

However, near them sitting in the water, were several shark-men shouting, arguing, and shaking their fearsome heads. Two of them were waving their flippers towards the shore, and as Orangey followed their direction with his eyes, he saw his three brothers looking wet and bedraggled, and extremely frightened. They had been dumped on the sand, still tied with seaweed, but the makeshift helmets had been removed and were lying close by.

Realising their presence, the shark-men swivelled round and looked at them, licking their gruesome lips in the expectation of extra feasts. Sylvie raised her voice and shouted at them, "Release those children, or my Father Neptune will have you hunted down and executed".

The shark-men foamed at the mouth with hate, their evil teeth showing against their dead grey skins. "My goodness", sneered one, "a brave little mermaid has come to save them, and threaten us, while the whole ocean knows that her father has departed to the other side of the world".

They all started laughing with a screaming whine in their voices, and in a combined rage, swam menacingly in the path of Sylvie and Orangey. Suddenly as from nowhere Sylvie produced a gleaming silver trident, and pointed it at the approaching horde. They stopped and sucked in their gills, breathing in and out with rapid movements showing their agitation.

Seeing his opportunity, Orangey leapt up in the water and dived onto the level sandy shore of the cavern. The shark-men hesitated and ground their teeth, considering which intruder to deal with first. Increasingly they became more agitated, uttering loud bleeping noises, as though to alert some other creatures.

As he lay in the sand, Orangey heard a hard clicking sound, and then the scraping of massive claws on rock. He glanced to his right and saw the three giant crabs moving towards him, ready to attack. He then realised that the odd bleeping noises from the sharkmen had indeed been an order to the crabs to join in the fray.

"Well I suppose I'm on some kind of land", he thought to himself, trying to bolster his courage, "although I'm really under the sea".

He removed his helmet and blinked his eyes, but nothing happened. He tried again, and then yet again, but the crabs sidled nearer and apparently unaffected by his powers. Only a few yards away now the leading crab, opened and closed its evil looking claws, ready to crush all that got in its way.

"Quick, take off your waterproof suit", shouted Sylvie while still swimming in the sea, "It may be deadening your magical ability". Frantically, Orangey pulled at the suit, but it was so skin tight that it wouldn't budge. The nearest crab opened its jaws, and swung a huge claw in a downward arc, in an attempt to crush him. Just in time the waterproof suit suddenly came away, he blinked, and powerful beams emitted from him and hit the monster. Firstly its massive claws fell apart at the joints, and crashed to the sand, and then its shell burst open along its back, spurting streams of grey-black matter from its insides. A final spasm and the remnants of innards oozed out onto the sand. It lay there twitching feebly.

Orangey aimed the lethal beams accurately at the two other crabs who were closing fast. They tried desperately to scramble back behind the rocks, slithering in their haste to hide, but as the beams struck, their shells erupted, pumping their grey-black slimy insides all over the cavern roof and walls.

While this was happening, Sylvie swam to the edge of the beach, expertly balancing her trident in front of her holding the shark-men at bay. They jabbered and ground their teeth, and in a seething rage swam towards Sylvie and Orangey. Altogether there were about nine or ten of them, with several others beginning to pop up from under the water. "Hold on tightly", shouted Orangey, as Sylvie thrust the trident into the sea only feet from the shark-men who were coming in fast. The leader opened his huge gaping mouth, clearly showing his evil pointed teeth. He snapped at the trident trying to bite off the prongs and render it useless.

Orangey blinked his eyes several times and immediately potent powerful currents of electricity ran down the handle of the trident. The water around them became warm, then hot, and then in next to no time it was boiling.

The shark-men screamed and thrashed about, their bodies were firstly coloured pink and then finally red, with the heat. Eventually shrinking and floating lifelessly out on the ebbing tide.

After his stalwart effort, Orangey sank to the sand feeling drained and weak, only then did he notice that Sylvie's hands were scorched and burnt badly, as she had bravely held the trident steady while the tremendous power had been surging through.

She saw his look of concern, "Don't worry", she said. "I'll be O.K.". Placing both of her hands in the sea, she sung softly, presently a shoal of brightly coloured fishes showed their heads, and nibbled at her hands. A soft sweet smelling substance was emitted from their mouths and coated Sylvie's hands. "Look", she whispered, "they'll be as right as rain in no time", and continued gently rubbing the creamy mixture into her skin.

Orangey loosed the seaweed from his brothers, who had been watching the events from close by. They stood there helplessly trying to support each other, as their legs had lost circulation.

"How will we ever manage to get back to the hotel?" asked Orangey dejectedly, "I'm sure they can't swim, and however will they breathe under water? They already look exhausted". "The best thing I can think of", answered Sylvie, "is to put the helmets back on their heads, and I'll ask my friends the dolphins to give them a ride on their backs".

She hummed sweetly into the sea, passing a message through the waves, this time the dolphins' heads appeared all around the shore, their happy mouths smiling a greeting. Some leapt right out of the water with happiness to see Sylvie, and she patted them all in turn.

In no time at all, they were heading back to the craggy rocks in style, holding on tightly to the dolphins' backs as they glided under the sea, and then going faster and faster as they shot to the surface.

Only a few minutes more and they reached the black rock where the boys had been captured. Carefully the dolphins landed the brothers on the soft sand of the beach, and then swam around making friendly blipping noises of goodbye.

At last Bluey, Greeny and Pinky, were beginning to recover from their ordeal, and stood happily on the shore waving goodbye to the dolphins after patting the clever fishes on their snouts as a token of thanks.

Before the boys set off along the beach to the hotel, Bluey asked, "How on earth did you find us under the sea" and then smiled as Pinky said, "Are you sure that is the right expression to use?". "You know what I mean", replied Bluey digging Pinky in the ribs, "we thought we were as good as dead didn't we?". Greeny joined in the conversation and added, "We never want to come to the seaside again either".

"Oh I don't know", said Orangey, "you'll remember the good things too, the tiny fishes who healed Sylvie's hands, and the clever dolphins who brought you back safely".

He then turned somewhat shyly to Sylvie and said "You mustn't forget our beautiful mermaid, whose bravery saved all our lives". Nodding in agreement the boys shook Sylvie's hand one by one, holding it gingerly, in case she still felt some pain. Then somewhat dejectedly but with a slight swagger as they had survived their unwanted adventure, they set off for the hotel.

Orangey stood for a while by the bleak rock, waved out to the last of the disappearing dolphins, and kissed Sylvie on the cheek. Tiny silver tears dropped onto his tunic, "Goodbye Orangey", she whispered, "even although it might be dangerous, please come back again, I'll guide you to the hidden treasure and we can open the treasure chest together".

"I promise to come back", replied Orangey, and then walked sadly along the beach following his brothers. The wind blew the salt spray off the sea, making him shiver. He hoped that the remainder of the holiday would be fun, but not so frightening.

Next day the sun shone, and the previous night's adventure all but forgotten.

ORANGEY AND THE SPACE BEINGS

O rangey decided to go to the wood one night alone, so he waited until his three brothers Bluey, Greeny and Pinky were fast asleep. Then he quietly opened the bedroom window, and flew out into the dark night.

As he flew across the lawn, he noticed that although the stars were visible, and the moon only partially obscured by cloud, it was extremely difficult to see very far in front of hint.

So he skirted the edge of the forest, and then headed inwards past the fairies' magic circle, where he saw the old barn owl sitting sentry. The owl seemed to want to speak to him, but Orangey flew on without stopping, intent on his own thoughts.

As he zoomed closer to the centre of the forest, he became aware of many broken branches, and badly flattened grass. Sitting under a damaged elm tree he saw a starling with a crumpled wing, fluttering helplessly. Lying nearby was a grey rabbit with its legs crushed, its eyes looking appealingly at Orangey. He stopped and blinked his eyes, once for the starling and then again for the injured rabbit. Immediately the bird's wing mended, and it flew happily into the forest with a loud chirrup. The rabbit's eyes lightened with thanks, and he hopped gratefully into the undergrowth to hide.

Some way further on the grass had turned yellow, and as the clouds cleared the moon for a moment, Orangey saw large circular tracks on the forest floor, becoming larger and larger. Then the grass colour changed to dark brown, and finally a scorched black. He pressed the button on his moonbeam torch, given to him by his cousin Goldie, the beam shone out brightly for nearly a hundred yards, lighting up the surrounding trees.

Roughly a hundred yards away but just out of the range of the torch beam, at the bottom of a slight slope, he could make out the outline of a glistening silver orb.

As he watched, four or five silvery figures came out of it, appearing to walk right through the outer shell, and then moved silently into the forest, coming towards him.

Orangey approached the figures, and raised the torch, shining it at the nearest image, the creature swung round, so that Orangey could see its bright green eyes looking at him intently. "Who are you?" asked Orangey, "and what do you want here?". A slit appeared under the eyes and a red forked tongue shot out and moved up and down, as a mechanically sounding voice replied, "Plere is this whace?" Orangey moved closer, "Plere is this whace?" droned the voice. "What are you saying?" asked Orangey.

The voice spoke again, "le are wost", it muttered in a lower tone. Suddenly Orangey understood the strange words, he realised that the words were being spoken with the first letter of each major word being put before the last. So he replied, "can I celp you?", the slit curved upwards into what was probably meant to be a smile.

Speaking in the same manner, Orangey said, "mou yust ake an madjustment on your speech computer", and then explained the reason. The slit opened again, but this time the forked tongue remained inside, so Orangey assumed it was a way of warning strangers before they were sure of their intentions, he hoped he had passed the test.

The voice sounding less mechanical replied, "thank you friend, we have now adjusted our speech computer as you suggested". Then a thin snake-like arm streaked out and shook Orangey's arm up and down in a form of greeting. It felt quite hot to the touch, but certainly a friendly power force came through as well.

The other figures crowded around Orangey in a semicircle, waving their skinny arms. The first figure who was probably the leader, spoke again, the slit curving slightly upwards, "Our craft developed engine trouble on the edge of your atmosphere", he explained. Pointing at the damage to the forest he continued, "We dropped nearly completely out of control in this forest area, and only just managed to avoid crashing into more trees with our emergency solar power full on, even so I'm afraid that the excess radiation has burnt up parts of the forest".

"Well it was an emergency, and I don't suppose it could have been avoided. Not everyone on this planet is aware of the damage they sometimes inflict on nature", Orangey replied with some fervour.

"Is it possible that you can help us?" asked the leader. "We are very slow moving and cumbersome in these suits that we have to wear in your atmosphere. If we explain our needs, perhaps you could help us to get them". "I'll certainly try", replied Orangey, "but you have landed in a country area near a small village, and we are unlikely to have what you require here".

The snake-like arms moved pointing to the other figures in turn, "Forgive my manners, my name is Orion, and these are Brion, Grion, Sion, and lastly Ariane", he said indicating a slightly smaller figure with penetrating green and amber eyes. The beings waved their arms, the slits in their helmets, that Orangey realised were not their actual heads, curved into that weird smile. "Please enter our craft, and we'll discuss our problems with you", invited Orion. "Certainly", replied Orangey, "but firstly I must introduce myself. I'm called Orangey, and you should also know that I am not entirely a normal human species". He sighed and continued, "Normal humans would probably be frightened by you and your spacecraft, but I am an elf, endowed with magical powers, which are not understood by ordinary human beings".

"That is excellent", said Orion, "It is fortunate for us that we met you first, I'm sure you will be able to help us". "Well firstly", answered Orangey, "I think it would be a good idea to hide your spacecraft". He blinked several times and fresh green branches sprouted out of the trees, covering the craft and making it all but invisible.

"That's very impressive", said Orion. "Wait", said Orangey, and blinked some more, this time the silver colour of the craft changed rapidly to a dark jade green. "That's better", smiled Orangey, "Now I don't believe even the witch could find it". "The witch?" queried Orion. "Oh I'll have to tell you more about her later", replied Orangey, noticing that the other beings had returned to the spacecraft, and somehow had disappeared into its interior, although he could see no sign of an entrance door.

Orion indicated to Orangey, and then guided his hand over the smooth almost polished surface, until it reached a spot that felt warm. It then became hot, and then just prior to becoming really burning hot, when Orangey was ready to snatch his hand away, a gentle power inside the space ship, gripped his hand and pulled him firmly through the outer shell.

The sensation was similar to climbing into a hot bath, and he felt cleansed, even with his clothes on. The interior smelt of fresh herbs with a strange but pleasant tang, and he found he could breathe easily.

The other beings were sitting around a table with a crystal of fabulous clarity hanging over it, giving out light, and from time to time shooting out laser beams in all directions. They beckoned him to sit down, and as he did so, the thought struck him that they seemed much smaller, and then it dawned on him that they had removed their special suits. They certainly look quite human except that their ears had extra large lobes, he thought. The only other noticeable difference was that their fingers were exceptionally long, while the skin of their faces were rather pale with a silvery hue to them. Their eyes gleamed and were completely green like Orion's, with the exception of Ariane's which he had already noticed, were flecked with amber.

He was offered a metallic jug with a flat spout, and was shown how to lift it up to his lips and draw in his breath lightly. A cool clear liquid touched his tongue, it tasted of honey, then tangerine, then banana, then chocolate, and finally of melon. He placed the jug back on the table with a satisfied smile on his face.

Orion grinned, "That's one of our better inventions. The clear liquid pours through a miniature computerised filter, and tastes of whatever your brain programmes it to". He continued, "By the look on your face you tried quite a few flavours without being aware of the secret".

"I'll try it again, if I may", said Orangey, thinking of the pink champagne cocktails he and his brothers had sneaked at the wedding where he had first met Goldie his cousin. He drank again, exactly like the champagne, he thought, and then a bubble went up his nose, and he sneezed. "Excuse me", he giggled, they all laughed too, its good to know that they have a sense of humour, he thought to himself, but I wonder what it's like living on their planet.

Altogether he decided that they were attractive people, not the gruesome green beings one usually visualised, with long feelers, and inhuman faces, ready to zap you with ray guns.

Orion was talking again, and pointing to a wafer thin

computer. He explained, "Our mini reactor failed first, and then so much power was required from the solar backup system, it nearly packed up as well".

He waved his arms in the direction of the computer screen, "You will note, that we need two separate forms of nuclear fuel, both of which will be radioactive, so you must be extremely careful". He beckoned to Ariane, who brought two containers to him. "We can supply you with these special canisters, which are supplied with a fluid gas, which both propels, and lightens them when in transit".

Orangey confidently picked up a slim metal pointer, and slid it across the computer screen, pressing a key, marked query one outline. "I will need more information about the type of fuels", he said. Orion pressed another key, and a formula flashed onto the screen, followed by another. Within seconds Orion pulled two clear printouts from the machine, printed on thin plastic sheets, and handed them to Orangey.

"If you cheek the formulae details with any supplies you may be able to obtain, it should be relatively easy to compare them for compatibility". Orangey looked at the print outs and asked, "Is this type of fuel available on our Earth planet?". Orion quickly checked the computer, "It appears you have something similar here, providing you manage to find us a similar fuel, we can make an adjustment in our power unit to enable us to return home".

Orangey mused for a moment or two, "Is it possible that one of you could accompany me?" he asked. Orion replied, "I'm afraid not, we are not capable of existing for long periods in your environment, and we would become more of a liability to you".

"Well that's clear", said Orangey, "I'm on my own, so I'll leave without any further delay. There's nothing else that I need to know is there?". He swung round ready to leave, "Oh", he said, as an afterthought, "Your spacecraft is well hidden, but as I am likely to be away for a relatively long while, I think I had better form an invisible shield over it so that it cannot be stumbled upon accidentally".

For the first time the beings frowned and looked perturbed, "We understood that earth creatures had not progressed far enough to be able to create an invisible shield", said Ariane. "Now you forget that I am a magic elf", Orangey replied, "otherwise I wouldn't be capable of carrying out this mission on your behalf". The frowns that creased their faces, changed to smiles. "Of course, you are quite correct, we had forgotten", they chorused. Then held out their slim hands to wish him good luck.

Soon Orangey was speeding on his way north through the night sky, he was delighted that the canisters felt so light and mobile, they even helped propel him forward much faster than his usual high speed.

Within minutes he touched down outside a huge nuclear power station, he glanced at the sign it read "KEEP OUT", and the skull and crossbones had been painted alongside.

Knowing exactly where he was making for, and silently thanking his father for encouraging his interest in science, he flew over the main fence, avoiding the reactor building, and made for a smaller structure nearby.

Without hesitating he squeezed down through an open air vent, and landed right into the centre of the building. He looked around and saw a massive steel door, he blinked three times and it swung open without triggering any alarms.

Inside it looked rather like a vault found in an old castle, but on either side were sealed steel drawers, he suspected lined with lead. Right in the centre of the floor was a huge computer complex, which was sending out shafts of light, and occasionally letting out soft bleeps, thoroughly convincing him that it was switched on and operative. He slid onto the seat opposite the computer screen, and after some experimentation managed to punch in the two formulae from the plastic sheets he had brought from the spacecraft.

With a flashing of electric power, the screen lit up, "Information Unavailable", he read. He blinked at the screen, invoking his magic means. He pressed the keys once more, and this time the formulae data was registered on the screen. He then blinked twice more, and activated the "obtain" key. The screen lit up with a succession of red symbols, finally a flashing light formed digits to indicate words, it read "Vault G18". As he withdrew the printout, he spotted a smaller red light flashing on and off on one of the sealed drawers. He looked closely and was relieved to see that it read G18.

He pushed the two containers in front of him, and concentrated on one small area on the vault, slowly it became warm, and then hot. He was using the same principle the space beings adopted to enter their craft. Before the metal actually glowed with heat, he pushed the canisters through the wall, with some ease.

When the containers were fully inside, he activated the extraction units by remote control, tapped out the reverse programme on the computer, and within minutes the fully loaded canisters were back in his hands.

He kept his fingers crossed that he had obtained the correct nuclear fuel, and confidently deactivated the computer. As he did so, a terrific noise vibrated throughout the whole building, he guessed that he had broken the alarm beam.

Next he heard a pack of guard dogs barking and howling near the main entrance, but luckily not near the building he was in. Almost immediately a siren screamed, coming nearer, waiting no longer he scrambled off the seat, and zoomed up the air vent, and poked his head out. Racing towards the building was a truck loaded with men in fallout suits, chased by the pack of maddened dogs.

Orangey shot into the air, flying quickly up into the dark night, going as high as he could manage, and was soon out of sight of the guards and the ferocious hounds.

Even with the weight of the fuel, the two canisters were surprisingly light, for which he was thankful. The unusual gas supplied by his space friends, propelled him and his load, with very little effort on his part, and the sound of the frantic dogs died into the distance.

He was delighted to find himself entering the outskirts of the wood in an amazingly short space of time. However, he became aware that if he stayed on this direct route, he would have to fly near the witch's cave. As he started to veer away, the witch's guard bats suddenly rose in a black chattering mass, surrounding him with their bodies.

Too late, he knew that Haggotty would shortly be alerted by their din that intruders were nearby. Hurriedly he flew by, but was surprised to catch sight of her leaving the cave on her broomstick with Spooks her cat clinging on for dear life.

"That's strange", he thought, "I've never seen her get mobile so rapidly, I wonder what she's up to?".

Seconds later, he landed safely by the side of the hidden spacecraft, and was pleased to note that everything appeared to be as he left it. He carefully placed the containers on the ground, and blinked three times to eliminate the protective barrier. Then he ran his hands over the exposed surface to find the warm spot, so that he could enter. It became rapidly warmer, and then got really hot, and he felt himself being drawn into the craft. With his free hand he reached out for the canisters, and found ... nothing. He glanced back, and saw Haggotty sitting on her broomstick, just behind him. Spooks her cat was sitting on one of the canisters, with his paws on the other, he had a silly smug look on his face, and shot his tail up in the air with glee, when he spotted Orangey's anguished expression.

Orangey couldn't prevent himself from being drawn into the interior of the craft, as he reached the inside, the five space beings rose from the table, and stood there expectantly. "Well", they asked hopefully, "I 'er got the fuel, but I 'er lost it", Orangey mumbled. Orion drew himself up to his full height, and looked quite menacingly at Orangey, "What do you mean, you lost it? Kindly explain", he ordered.

Orangey quickly told them about the witch, and her evil powers, and how she had followed him to the spacecraft and stolen the canisters. "You know I have an idea that she may have been watching us, all along", added Orangey. "Do you know where she might store the containers?" asked Orion. "I can only guess, probably back at her cave", answered Orangey. "I've heard tell that it goes right back into the mountain, and would be hidden well out of sight". Orion pursed his thin lips together, and mused, "I think we might be able to thwart her yet. Many years ago on our planet we also suffered the evil of similar witches, and we might have a surprise or two in store for her".

He beckoned to Ariane who came nearer, he then continued to outline a plan. "If Ariane removes her space suit, and we supply her with a temporary means of breathing in your atmosphere, can you help her to fly?". "I think so", said Orangey. "Good", replied Orion, "she knows many methods of defeating witches. Between you it's possible you may be able to return our fuel".

Orangey nodded agreement, and shortly was flying towards the witch's cave, towing Ariane behind. They landed about a hundred years or so from the entrance, as Orangey did not want to take the risk of alerting the witch's bats again. "What exactly is the plan?" asked

Orangey as they landed. "Haggotty is extremely powerful, and really dangerous, so we must be very careful".

Ariane began to explain the plan, "I have these tiny but effective capsules which emit a heavy burning smoke, it smells disgusting like flesh smouldering, and is capable of choking someone in seconds". She looked at Orangey with her beautiful green eyes, "Furthermore, witches are traditionally afraid of being burnt at the stake, and the fear impairs their evil powers".

Orangey nodded in agreement as Ariane continued whispering, "Before I pump it into the cave, you must disguise me as a witch from another area. If you use your magic well, she'll never tell the difference, and I'll pretend that I've just escaped being burnt myself, and that I believe the persons concerned are searching out and burning any witches they find".

Orangey blinked his eyes and in a trice Ariane was whisked away, and in her place stood a nasty old crone, who looked even more awful than Haggotty herself.

The second witch spoke in a broken cackle, difficult to understand. Orangey listened intently as she mumbled, "I'll attract her attention, and while she and I discuss the best way of avoiding capture, you can creep into her cave and retrieve the canisters". As soon as Ariane approached the mouth of the cave, all bedlam broke out, as the bats disturbed for the second time that night, squawked and chattered hysterically as she hurriedly positioned the capsules, and then activated them.

Firstly Spooks came bounding out of the cave, his eyes

blood red and streaming with tears, shortly followed by the witch, who was holding a scarf around her mouth and eyes. She stumbled and leant against a tree coughing, she looked up through misty eyes, and saw Ariane dressed as a witch, sitting on a tree trunk chanting to herself.

"Who are you?", hissed the witch, Ariane continued chanting, "Oh witch of these woods, and friend of her sisters", she added spying Haggotty's malevolent face, "I have travelled many miles from my home to warn you that many wickedly minded men are scouring the area, in an attempt to hunt out any witches, and evil spirits".

Looking directly at Spooks she repeated, "evil spirits, and are burning to death all they find, I have only just managed to escape myself, but my broomstick was destroyed by the fire". "How terrible", replied Haggotty, looking at Ariane in her scorched and charred clothes. "Where can we hide, they must be close by, as my cave is filled with foul smelling smoke".

"I'm afraid that I have some internal injuries, so I can only walk slowly", said Ariane. "However, on the way here I did notice a small cave under the waterfall where we can hide, I think we'd better walk as if we fly on your broomstick we could easily be seen", she added craftily.

"Aha", echoed Haggotty, "I expect my broomstick is charred to nothing back there in the cave. Yes, we must walk". As they made their way slowly to the river, Orangey with a mask over his face, slipped into the witch's cave. Even with the witch out of the way, he found himself wishing to get the job done speedily. He trod on a pile of old bones, and shivered, wondering where they had come from, and whose they were. Luckily he found the canisters easily, propped up against the witch's black iron pot, he grabbed them and flew hastily back to the spacecraft.

Orion and his friends were waiting, and he left them working on the fuel system, as he sped off into the forest, to follow Ariane and the witch, as they neared the waterfall.

He was trying to work out a plan, to get Ariane away from the witch, without having to confront her, and challenge her evil magic, when suddenly he heard a squeak, then a cough, followed by a gruff meow. Looking to his right just off the path he espied Spooks, sitting rubbing his eyes with his paws. Orangey blinked and Spooks fell over into a deep sleep without another sound.

Orangey picked him up deftly, and shot off, flying quickly until he was well in front of the toiling witches. He selected a spot, and placed him on the path, where they would pass, on their way to the river. As they eventually came round the bend, they saw Spooks lying on the ground with his eyes tightly closed, apparently dead. The witch rushed up to him, screeching, "They've killed him, they've killed my lovely cat. What wicked creatures could have done this?". While she was jumping up and down with rage, Ariane slipped unnoticed behind a tree, and was soon being towed by Orangey back to her friends.

They both giggled, "She really fell for that", whispered Ariane, "what a good idea". As they landed they saw that the craft had already been moved a few yards, and all of the covering foliage had been removed. It looked ready to depart.

Looking at Ariane's tatty witch's clothing Orangey said, "I'd better change you back, or your friends might not let you on the spacecraft with them". He blinked his eyes, and Ariane stood there smiling, she held out her long arms and gave him a hug. It gave him a real thrill, being hugged by a creature from outer space. She looked at him with her bright green eyes, and murmured, "We'll never forget your help". She moved towards the spaceship and Orangey saw that the others led by Orion were standing watching. They shook his hand in turn, and then entered the craft, "Goodbye and thank you", they shouted as they disappeared into its depths.

Orangey heard just a slight whooshing sound, and the craft rose effortlessly into the air, hung there for a moment, and then sped away, in a few seconds it was out of sight. Orangey blinked away a tear, and walked slowly home through the forest he knew so well.

But back at the river things were not so quiet. Haggotty picked up the still figure of Spooks, and wiped away a tear. The cat slowly opened one eye, and looked up at her wondering why he was being carried. "You revolting creature", she stormed dropping him onto the hard ground. "You were only pretending to be dead to give me a fright". "Oh no I wasn't", wailed the cat, "I was sitting there rubbing my eyes, when suddenly I felt terribly tired". "Excuses, excuses ...", hissed the witch, "I'll make you pay for this, getting me all worried for nothing. By the way where's the other witch?", she suddenly exclaimed. "She was talking about witches being hunted and burnt, but come to think of it, they don't do that anymore. What am I thinking about?" she snarled at Spooks, "I think there's something funny going on here'". "What are you talking about?" squeaked Spooks, "I didn't see another witch". "You useless animal you never see anything, what help are you to me? Why do I bother to feed you?". Spooks eyes opened in horror, "What, no more food?", he meowed plaintively.

Haggotty ignored Spooks and pondered for a moment, "I think we've been duped", she stormed. With those words she automatically got astride her broomstick to shoot away, but of course it wasn't there. "I've left it in the cave in all that smoke", she snapped at Spooks. "Bones and tricks will bring back sticks", she chanted. Within seconds her broomstick came zooming through the air straight at them, it slowed down, but hit Spooks with a loud whack, as it landed. "I think you did that on purpose", wailed Spooks. Haggotty didn't answer, but sped off at great speed, "Wait for me", meowed Spooks pitifully, then lolloped off behind the flying witch, his tail dragging on the ground.

ORANGEY CONFRONTS
HAGGOTTY THE WITCH

Orangey had an uneasy feeling about the forest; as he set off with his brothers Bluey, Greeny and Pinky for their rendezvous with Caramilla and her fairy sisters. It was somehow quite different from normal, for one thing it was unusually quiet, and a feeling of dramatic things to come haunted him.

As they flew steadily towards the magic circle they all began to realise that something was afoot; it had never been so quiet before. Even at night they would hear the hoot of the old barn owl, or a chirp from a starling or other forest bird. But tonight there was no sign of a solitary rabbit hopping into the bushes, a single dormouse scampering off into the undergrowth, or a cheeky squirrel sitting on a branch eating nuts.

The only animals in sight were a handful of deer, and they were all moving in the direction of the gamekeeper's cottage on the far side of the wood.

When they landed by the edge of the magic circle all eleven fairies were waiting for them. Caramilla their leader appeared very agitated, nothing like her normal happy smiling self, and the glum looks on the faces of her sisters told the same story.

Caramilla smiled fleetingly and said, "I'm so glad you have arrived, we have some bad news I am afraid". She then handed Orangey a piece of dried bark with a message written on it in congealed bats' blood.

He read the message aloud, "By command of Haggotty the senior witch in the area of Erebus, BEWARE all Elves and Fairies must leave the forest forthwith, taking the animals with you".

In a sombre trembling voice Caramilla went on to explain that the day following receipt of the message, the witch's raven had brought another demand, which was so terrible, she couldn't bring herself to talk about it.

Orangey took the second piece of bark in his hands and read the decree in loud ringing tones, as though to defy the witch's wishes. It read "Anyone defying my command will suffer the following punishment: Fairies to have their wings severed, and then to be tied to logs and set adrift on the river as a warning to others". Even Orangey could not continue reading out the dreadful details, so gave the others the barest inkling of her demands as follows. It included that if her commands were not met within forty-eight hours, and if any animals were found grazing within a ten-mile radius of her cave they would be forcibly rounded up, and driven out of the forest. Furthermore some would be slaughtered and sold to the pet food shops in the area, as meat for cats and dogs.

Caramilla sobbed and dabbed a tiny crystal tear from her eye, "There is a footnote", she whispered to Orangey, "Yes I will read that as well", he agreed. "It says that the rats have been excluded from this decree as they have sworn allegiance to the witch".

There was a stunned silence as he finished, then fairy number five, Evangeline, whispered, "What ever can we do? The forest has always been our home, we have nowhere else to go". Orangey got to his feet with a fierce and determined look on his face, he announced, "To protect our animals, and their homes, we'll have to challenge the witch, or she'll change the shape of the forest forever".

The fairies huddled together speaking among themselves, and then Caramilla voiced their fears. "There are so few of us, and Haggotty's so powerful, she'll call on the help of evil spirits, and bring in the hobgoblins and the nastiest gnomes". She paused for breath, and they shuddered, as she continued, "She'll have a vast army, and there are more than two hundred hobgoblins, and that's not counting the gnomes. It's so frightening". Tiny crystal tears ran down her cheeks, and then all of the other fairies joined in, weeping and sobbing.

"It will be difficult and dangerous", agreed Orangey, "but we'll have to plan a campaign to beat her. We'll ask the animals for their support". "After all", he continued, "there's many hundreds of them, we'll muster quite a force". "It's worth a try I suppose", Caramilla spoke up, "but the animals are gentle, and I don't think they'll make very good fighters".

"That's all true", said Orangey, "but we'll organise them to dig pits, and set traps along the paths leading to the witch's cave, and we'll get the old owl and the other birds to alert us of any coming danger". "It might work, but if it doesn't, we're all doomed", Caramilla's voice shook as she spoke, and she started crying again.

"Now please don't cry anymore", appealed Bluey, "you know how I hate you girls crying". The fairies looked at Bluey, and then Evangeline giggled, and said, "Oh Bluey, you're such a big softy, but you do make us laugh, so whatever happens, we'll try not to cry anymore, just for you".

Bluey blushed, looking more like Pinky for an instant. Greeny added "None of us like to hear you girls crying; anyway we can't stand by and see all of us driven from the forest, without making an effort to help". Greeny rarely made such a long speech, usually only thinking deeply about matters, but not often expressing his feelings.

So that night the elves and the fairies toured the wood talking to the animals that were left, and explaining to them how they could all help. The old owl who missed nothing, soon joined them and made plans to enlist the help of the forest birds, of which there were plenty. They also spoke to the Happy Gnome, and asked him to gather all of his fellow gnomes, so that they could join in and help the cause.

After much hard work, and lots of magic, all of the paths

leading to the witch's cave were soon crisscrossed with open pits, covered with leaves and twigs to disguise them. Above the paths, hanging traps with woven hemp were suspended at strategic points.

By morning most of the work had been completed, and Caramilla was left in charge, while Orangey and his brothers returned home. It was necessary that they set off for school at the normal time in the morning. Of course most of you know by now, that although during the day they looked just like any other small boys, they were really elves. This is a closely guarded secret that can never be divulged to grownups, as they would find it difficult to understand. That day in school, the deputy headmistress, Miss Timson-Jones, took the class in a history lesson; and her boring account of the combined forces of the Austrian and French armies, drawn up against the much smaller British army in the fifteenth century, reminded Orangey of the one-sided situation he and the fairies found themselves in against the witch and her followers.

Miss Timson-Jones twitched her long nose, and looked down it at Orangey. "Ossie Rangey", she commanded, "What was the name of the British General, at the battle of Blenheim Forest in 1823?". Coming out of a daydream with a start, he replied without thinking, "Er Storming Norman, Miss". "What rubbish", she hissed, "Remain after class is dismissed, and write out two hundred times, I must pay attention in class".

That afternoon Orangey arrived back home much later than his brothers, and although he thought he was probably suffering from writer's cramp, went immediately to his father's workshop to prepare his second part of the plan of attack.

Firstly he pondered with the idea of carving some huge ogres, similar to the tactics he had used before when he'd successfully set a trap for his horrid schoolmistress, and Haggotty the witch.

After due consideration, he decided against it, partly because it would be difficult to explain the presence of several giants to his father, who was likely to use the workshop over the weekend, on his return from work as a gardener. However, he did carve a couple of dozen small figures in the likeness of the elves and fairies which he was pleased to see, looked extremely lifelike.

He planned to place them in the forest at the head of his meagre forces, as at a slight distance it would he difficult to tell them apart from the real ones.

An hour or so after their parents had gone to bed, Orangey led his brothers out of the bedroom window and headed for the wood. They were joined by the old barn owl, who guided them to a different meeting place. He hooted that a scouting party of hobgoblins had been seen lurking near their usual rendezvous.

The fairy sisters looked rather wan and tired after their efforts to prepare the animals against the witch's attack, but were delighted to see Orangey and his brothers arrive. They were thrilled with the figurines that Orangey had carved, and thought it was a super idea to use them as decoys.

Before any further discussion took place, Orangey asked the owl to fly to Goldie's house, and ask her to meet them in the forest as soon as possible. He was hoping that her extra magic powers would help tip the balance in their favour.

With his unerring knowledge of the forest the owl returned within a few minutes, to report that Goldie would be joining them shortly. He added that she had some preparations of her own to complete first.

In the meanwhile, Orangey and Caramilla rechecked the pits and traps, and agreed on a password, in case any of the witch's hobgoblins tried to pass themselves off as elves in the dark. They had decided to use the word "Protector", and this was circulated to all of the friendly elves and animals.

It was becoming chilly around 1.00am when the owl flew back from one of his sorties, and settled on a branch just above them. Apparently he had noticed a great deal of movement between the wood and the river, and told of hundreds of hobgoblins and aggressive gnomes lining up in massed legions, preparing to attack.

Orangey had already found out that trying to pass some of his magic powers on to his brothers was a very tricky business, and just didn't work. So he compromised by giving them some limited protection against the witch's black magic.

Having passed on his latest information, the owl perched in his sentry position on the tallest oak, and stared with unblinking eyes into the darkness for signs of the enemy.

Presently a tiny golden light, growing brighter all the time, hovered above, and then descended into their midst. It was Goldie, and she was carrying an armful of mirrors and polished metal plates. They varied in size and conformation, being a mixture of convex and concave, already moonbeams were shooting from them, as she landed. She smiled and said softly, "Hello everyone", they all smiled and nodded in return. "Those look most interesting", said Orangey, pointing to the mirrors, "What are they for?". I've been studying the moon and star formations and working out how best to harness their reflective light beams". Goldie replied, "I hope to be able to use them to our advantage, and confuse the witch's vanguard", she continued. "That's a great idea", said Orangey, "I hope it works, as we're about as ready as we'll ever be". He raised his voice slightly, talking to everyone, "Let's line up with the river protecting our left flank, and the waterfall behind us".

Before they could move, the owl sailed in from yet another sortie, to say that there had been more activity at the rear of the witch's forces, but in the dark even he had been unable to make out exactly what the reason was. "Something very large I think", he hooted, "because of its size, and it's so slow moving, it could be a tank brigade". "That's not possible", retorted Orangey, "with tanks moving, we'd have heard the noise all over the forest, and it's as quiet as the ...", he considered saying the grave, but changed his mind, "It's very quiet", he repeated. "Anyway, whatever it is, we must get into position, and without further delay". He waved to them to follow him.

So slowly and making as little noise as possible they made

their way to the riverbank. The brothers placed the carved statuettes in two rows in front of their positions, and then Goldie with her mirrors, they then placed themselves just behind, ready to assist her if needed. The others came up the rear, the elves and gnomes in a position to control the animals, who were kept right at the back for their own safety. Caramilla and her fairy band fluttered nearby, ready to come to the aid of any hard pressed section of the force.

When they were all in place, Orangey blinked his eyes, and formed an invisible, completely transparent protective shield at the front of his band. He trusted that it would hold against the witch's evil spirits, realising that although it was invisible to most, she would be able to see it. He sincerely hoped that her followers wouldn't, and might become disheartened if they couldn't break through the barrier.

Progressively the night chill had turned to a strange oppressive heat, with a haze of dark grey cloud hemming them in tightly to their chosen positions. The black cloud was hanging closely around the moon, allowing very little light to see by. Certainly nothing like enough for Goldie to project the beams from her mirrors.

They waited in silence, not a word being uttered, and despite the closeness, when an eerie sound echoed through the forest, Pinky shivered with fear, "What's that?", he whispered. No one answered, as they were all wrapped up in their own worries, and it was too strange a noise to have been made by any animals they knew.

Sitting wondering what type of creature uttered such weird noises, they remained baffled, when suddenly without any further warning, several great flying shapes appeared overhead. Moving slowly through the night darkness, they edged closer, their massive mouths opened, and long spurts of red fire shot out. The stream of flame burned large smoking holes in the protective barrier, and it started to melt.

As the horrendous creatures swung round, they were all horrified to see them hovering directly over them. Seven huge dragons, their backs covered in slime, with scaly overlapping plates protecting their flapping wings.

Diving in closer for a second attack, they emitted long flaming darts right into the centre of the shield, this time holes appeared as the melting progressed, but somehow it's magic held it together.

In the background and not far from the overhanging trees, they spotted Haggotty dancing up and down, waving her arms aloft, and shouting out frenzied instructions to the hobgoblins and gnomes to attack.

Spooks, her cat, was sitting on her broomstick which was suspended in the air, growling like a dog, and showing his sharp yellow teeth. The hair on his back was standing up in ghastly black bristles that gleamed a warning.

Orangey motioned to the owl, who hooted loudly, and at this command thousands of birds of all shapes and sizes flew out of the night sky, each one dropping a mouthful of water, which combined to form a massive deluge of water, which poured down over the dragons, reducing their fire power to a few flickers, and then doused the barrier.

The dragons veered away to recharge their fiery breath, and as they wheeled round, Orangey signalled to the owl again, who led in a second wave of birds to where the dragons were landing, and gave them a further drenching.

"Those I believe are your tanks", shouted Orangey above the din, "but they're just as lethal". The owl dipped his wings and sped off into the forest.

The constant stream of water directed accurately by the birds had reduced the firepower of the dragons to columns of steam. Orangey's small army let out a cheer of triumph, but this was cut short, as with horror they saw Haggotty unleash her horde of hobgoblins. They ran in a screaming mob to the unseen barrier and started waving their clubs wildly, battering it unmercifully.

Through the lower section of the shield, they could make out the fearsome twisted faces of the goblins, who were gnashing their teeth, and uttering blood curdling cries.

Quickly taking advantage of the deteriorating condition of the barrier, Orangey blinked his eyes, and it immediately began to melt rapidly into mountains of hot sticky burning plastic. It fell in huge splodges and engulfed the goblins, trapping most of them in scorching twists of melting debris.

Only a few managed to escape and ran terrified into the forest, towards the witch's cave, there they were caught in traps, or catapulted screaming into the pits.

Before the elves and fairies had time to rejoice this further victory, the dragons appeared again overhead, spitting out more fire, and now they were without the protective screen, the fairies and friends were extremely vulnerable, and likely to be burnt to death.

Orangey shouted the order to retreat, and just in time they fell back, and avoided the flames from the dragons' breath. However the two rows of carved figures, knocked over by the mad dash of the hobgoblins, were reduced to ashes.

The brave little birds dived in repeatedly, replenishing their water from the river, and raining it down on the flying dragons, until they wheeled away unable to produce their second burst of fire.

The unwieldy dragons flapped wearily back to the rear of the witch's depleted forces, to obtain time to regain their fiery breath.

"So far, so good", shouted Orangey to his brothers, "but unless we can get rid of the dragons for good, they are going to return and burn us alive".

It was obvious that one more attack might well defeat them, as although they had considerably lessened the numbers of Haggotty's army, they had lost the protective barrier, and the two rows of defending figures. They were of course still dramatically outnumbered, and as they looked a fresh wave of attackers swept towards them.

On came the remnants of the hobgoblin horde, their numbers increased by a gang of howling gnomes. The witch screamed a curse into the wind, and suddenly hundreds of fierce rats, some as big as Spooks himself, raced towards them.

At last the clouds moved from in front of the moon, and its bright beams shone streaks of light through the trees. Immediately Goldie and her helpers angled the mirrors to divert the rays, and direct them into the evil eyes of the oncoming assailants.

She had used her knowledge well, and as the final strands of cloud left the moon, the vastly magnified beams took their toll, flashing into the eyes of the rats, blinding and confusing them, and making them lose their sense of direction, as they surged forward, snarling and grinding their teeth. Nevertheless, the sheer weight of numbers enabled them to close in on Orangey's elves and few loyal gnomes, snapping and tearing at anything in their path.

At that precise moment the barn owl returned leading his flock of larger birds, this time with beaks and talons outstretched, they tore into the unprotected backs of the advancing rats, ripping and tearing until blood ran everywhere.

A terrible battle ensued, with Haggotty dancing with rage in the rear, and egging on her attacking forces. Spooks her cat was running up and down with the hairs on his back now raised several inches, but not doing much else.

The fairies flew in like streaks of light, darting in and out of the fray, encouraging the birds, and halting a good proportion of the rats by magic. They waved their tiny wands in unison, and the nearest rats slowed, their legs began to crumple and their teeth dropped out, showering the earth with red edged white pearl molars.

Seeing clouds of black bats streaming across the sky to join the battle, Orangey and Goldie sped into the thick of the fighting. Hard on the heels of the bats, came the newly revived dragons, in an effort to aid the failing rats.

Combining almost the last of their magic powers, Orangey and Goldie created another invisible barrier, giving the remainder of their force time to retreat, and take cover under the waterfall.

Unfortunately this barrier was rather weak, and held for only a short while, as the witch was increasing her evil power all the time. Then abruptly, the barricade disintegrated, and Orangey and Goldie found themselves surrounded by the witch's army.

The bats and dragons hovered overhead waiting for the order for the final strike, and on the ground the remnants of the rat army had eventually managed to encircle them. The remaining jabbering hobgoblins waved their weapons with unconcealed glee at the capture of the leaders of the opposing side.

Haggotty held up her hand with its long dirty pointed nails, "Surrender or die", she hissed. With the tremendous effort of the conflict, Orangey and Goldie realised that their magic powers were drained. So there was little else they could do but agree. "We will surrender", declared Orangey, "providing you allow my brothers, and the fairy sisters to go free".

Haggotty considered this for a moment, and decided that with Orangey and Goldie captured, she could do whatever she wanted with the others later. So she cackled "I agree, but you and Goldie must give up your magic powers to me without delay". They did not trust her, but had no alternative, so Orangey turned sadly to Goldie, and took her hands and held them tightly, trying to smile.

"Don't they look beautiful together", chanted the witch. "Separate them at once and tie their legs to these logs". As if to prove her great power, she struck two nearby trees with her sharp nails, sparks flew in all directions, and the trunks crashed to the ground, cut right through the middle in seconds.

Grinning horribly, the two biggest hobgoblins rushed forward with ropes in their hands, ready to bind the couple to the fallen logs. "Hurry up now, tie them well, and throw them in the river, as I promised to anyone defying me". She danced up and down with sheer glee, gloating over the doomed pair.

Without warning a flock of bats overhead parted, screaming in alarm, and then flew backwards and forward in terrible agitation. The winged dragons flapped nearer to the ground, and then soared up again, looking into the darkness.

Down through the atmosphere a formation of rotating silver orbs descended rapidly, hovering over them. As they got even nearer, they slowed and spun slightly in the air just above the trees, the heat from their engine units scorching the undergrowth.

The dragons closed on the orbs, and projected bursts of fire directly at them. As if nothing had happened, the orbs rotated slowly, getting their range, and shot out invisible streaks of supercharged electrical power. It tore into the dragons, reducing them to shreds, the powerful beams were then pinpointed accurately onto the rats, who shrivelled and burnt to embers. The remaining goblins suffered the same fate, as the incredibly concentrated rays then moved to the witch's broomstick.

It burst into flames, scorching Spooks, and charring his fur, he screeched and looked for help from the witch. Ignoring him, she gibbered and foamed at the mouth, with the shock of seeing her army annihilated in a few seconds. She dropped to the ground, covering herself with her magic cloak, and disappeared into the forest.

The leading craft landed without a sound, scattering the lurking bats in all directions. It remained stationary for several seconds, before five familiar figures appeared through the outer shell of the spaceship.

The leading pair were Orion and Ariane, clad in their earth suits, the slits in their helmets gave an upward turn in a smile of recognition. They held out their long arms and pumped Orangey's hand up and down vigorously. Orangey introduced Goldie to all five in turn, and they shook her hand up and down as well.

Grinning with relief, Orangey said, "Before you meet my brothers and the fairies, I must know how you were aware of our sad plight". Orion's smile grew, "Ever since you helped us, when we were stranded, we've kept a small insert on our computer scanning screen, and whenever we fly over your forest area, we plot your movements". He produced a silver model of the aircraft, and handed it to Orangey, "This time we were on our way to see you with a token of our thanks, and as soon as we received clearance from our control unit, came to your aid".

Orangey just nodded with pleasure, then he noticed the owl sitting on a tree gazing at the newcomers. "Come over here", he suggested. The owl winged over, and perched on a branch just above their heads, not certain of the strangers reaction.

Orangey gestured to Orion and said, "Please meet our good friend and ally, without his leadership in rallying the birds to confront the witch, and her wicked followers, I don't know what we would have done".

"We saw some of the fighting on the screen", replied Orion, "It must be worthwhile standing up for a cause when you have such staunch allies".

The old owl swelled with pride to nearly twice his size, fluffing out his feathers, when Orion placed a silver orb around his neck. "If you use this properly, it will guide you safely through the dark nights", he said earnestly.

The owl felt very proud, but didn't mention that he could already fly through the darkest forest without getting lost.

A noise from behind them, and then gasps of amazement alerted them to the fact that Orangey's brothers, and the fairies, had returned from their hiding place under the waterfall.

Thirty minutes after Orangey and Goldie had introduced everyone to each other, they watched the silver orb rotate in the sky, and fly in an arc towards the moon. Just for a moment it was difficult to tell it apart from the stars, until finally it disappeared into the softened blue of the early dawn.

ORANGEY MEETS THE ICE QUEEN

It was midwinter and the pure white snow lay in great frozen drifts on the forest floor, as Orangey and his three brothers crunched across it, leaving glistening footprints as they walked. The moon peered eerily from behind scurrying clouds, helping them to find the path through the wood to the side of the lake.

Usually they flew when they visited the forest, but because of the extreme cold, they had decided to walk to keep themselves warm. Orangey and his three brothers were really elves, but appeared to be normal small boys to their parents and other adults. Only Orangey was somewhat different as he was a 'magic elf', and his strange powers had helped them out of trouble on many occasions.

Soon they reached a fallen tree trunk that lay at an acute angle to the lake, its surface covered with frosty snow and ice. One by one they hopped onto it and slid down its entire length, gathering speed until they shot out onto the frozen lake, skidding over its slippery surface. It was an ideal starting point to speed skate across the ice, and in the pale light of the moon's rays, they noticed several tiny figures in the distance, flitting over the ice. As they got nearer they recognised their friends the fairies, and shouting out with glee, raced over to join them.

Puffing with exertion, they gasped, "We didn't know that you liked to skate. How about having a race to the other side of the lake?". Caramilla the fairies' beautiful leader turned and smiled at them, but before she could reply, they saw a glowing golden light appear over the treetops and come swiftly toward them. "Why I believe it's our cousin Goldie", exclaimed Bluey, "Now we're all here together we can have a terrific time". Goldie landed carefully near them, not wanting to slip; she was dressed in a one-piece ski outfit made of gold lame, with matching boots that glinted as she moved. "Hello cousin", greeted Orangey, "we've decided to have a race right across the lake. Do you want to join in?". "Why certainly", replied Goldie, shaking the fresh snow from her blonde ringlets, she smiled a welcome, and then added, "I think you should give us girls at least ten yards start, after all we are much smaller, especially Caramilla and the other fairies". Fairy no. 4 looked at Bluey shyly and giggled, "We don't want you to catch us up too quickly you know". "Well alright, we'll agree to that", said Orangey. "We'll form up in two lines, with you girls ten yards in front, mind you who'll give the order to start", he added. "How about me?", whispered a quiet voice. They all looked up to see that the Happy Gnome had crept up-on them unseen, and was standing nearby dressed in a huge fur coat, hanging right down to his ankles. "Don't you want to join in the race?", asked Bluey. "Well not really", he replied, "you see I promised to return this fur coat to the grizzled fox tonight, as he got it ripped while he was being chased by some silly dogs, who should have known better. You see I've just repaired it for him". "He'll be jolly cold without it in this weather", said Greeny, "you'd better hurry and take it back to him, mind you it looks miles too big on you". The fairies giggled and said, "It's a wonder you didn't trip over it and break your neck". A troubled look came over the gnome's face, and he winced slightly as he spoke in an even softer voice, and murmured, "Well you are nearly right, I did trip and sprain my ankle, and that's why I can't race with you".

"Come along now it's getting jolly cold standing here talking", interrupted Bluey, "let's get on with the race without any more discussion". So without further ado, they lined up ready to race, "Now, one, two, three, and off", shouted the Happy Gnome, recovering his normal voice.

They all sped off, careering over the ice. By the time they had reached the centre of the lake, Orangey and his brothers had nearly caught up with Goldie and the fairies, when suddenly without warning there was an almighty crack, and the ice gave way, sending them sliding helplessly into the cold waters of the lake. They found themselves going faster and faster into a wall of solid ice, but amazingly before the icy block reached them, it materialised into a slippery chute, which catapulted them right to the bottom of the lake. As they appeared to be certain to be crushed against another ice wall, an archway appeared, allowing them to slide unharmed into a cavern ringed with sparkling coloured icicles.

The brothers and the fairies had fallen in very untidy heaps on top of one another, recovering their breath, they gazed around in wonder at the massive pillars of differently coloured ice. Some of them rose from the ground in pointed shapes similar to warriors' swords. Others hung down from the high ceiling like menacing stalactites, threatening to fall and crush them. As they adjusted their eyes to the bright light, the giant icicles changed colour, from blue to red, then to green, orange to purple, and then mixed together into a gigantic ice rainbow.

They slowly got to their feet, gazing at the breathless raw beauty before them. "Have you ever seen anything like this before", breathed Goldie, helping Caramilla to regain her balance. "Wait a minute, is anyone hurt?", asked Orangey. They gingerly felt their arms and legs, "We think we're OK", they replied, and considering the speed at which they had been hurtled into the cavern, it was hard to credit that they were all quite unharmed. Getting over the initial shock Goldie asked, "I wonder where we are?" Orangey looked round the ice chamber, "It's a sort of underground cave, but made of solid ice", he replied. "And it's jolly cold", added Bluey.

Before they could decide what to do next, sounds of softly playing music, slowly swelled in volume, becoming louder and louder, until it was deafening. They looked towards the far end of the cavern, where the sound was so incredibly loud it was actually vibrating the icicles, creating minor shockwaves. These seemed to attack them, causing them to become disorientated, they placed their hands over their ears, trying to shut out the increasing tumult, then huddled together for comfort.

The music stopped abruptly as the wall parted like a curtain in the cinema, and sitting there on a throne studied with rubies, emeralds and diamonds, was a beautiful but haughty woman looking at them disdainfully. In one hand she held a sceptre that sent shafts of light shooting out into the cavern, in the form of transient rockets, showering multicoloured sparks in huge arcs of flame, and then retreating back into the sceptre only to be fired out again and again. In a clear majestic voice the woman spoke to them saying, "You are in my kingdom, my kingdom of ice and snow, I am the Ice Queen, and you will now do as I command". She rose to her feet, tall and threatening, her robes aglow with precious stones, sending out glints of harsh light, hurting their eyes. She spoke again, "You will all remain here to help in our perpetual tasks", she commanded, "there is much to be done". She then directed the shafts of light from the sceptre onto the walls of the cavern, hidden sliding doors opened without a sound, and a myriad of strange and frightening creatures crouched lurking at every entrance, their eyes darting over the group of frightened fairies and elves. Some had weird animal-like shapes and were covered in matted hair. Some were part animal with human heads, and many others crowding behind were giant versions of deformed gnomes and hobgoblins. The fearsome creatures stood quite mute, the only constant feature they shared was a crown of blue crystals on their heads, that continually moved like snakes wriggling on rocks, so although the creatures were motionless, the movement on their heads never ceased, the crystals seeming to have a life of their own.

Slowly recovering from the additional shock of being surrounded by fierce werewolf-looking beings of uncertain origin, Orangey regained his poise and started to speak. The Queen gestured to him angrily to be quiet, and said, "If you are wondering how to escape from my kingdom, I must tell you that no one has ever been able to evade our guards and leave us". She paused looking at them shivering in front of her, "If you don't all agree to work for me you will remain here encased in ice forever; mind you", she boasted, "everyone finally agrees, and is given a headdress of blue crystals, through which I will direct my commands which must be obeyed immediately, or shockwaves of intense pain will shoot through your heads; bringing madness if not ceased within a certain time".

Surprisingly she then changed her tone, to one of conciliation, "But come now, firstly one of my lieutenants will show you my wonderful kingdom, and the essential work that we do, and perhaps you will be happy to join us with only friendly persuasion". "Fat chance", thought Orangey, ready to argue, but one of the smaller creatures who was still nearly six feet tall, held out its hand and motioned them to follow. They passed through one of the larger arches into a corridor. Then allowed themselves to be ushered along it until they reached many more passageways leading off into all directions like the radius of the sun. The first led into a spacious chamber which smelt of the fragrance of wild flowers, and in the ceiling they could see the roots and lower stems of many early spring flowers. "These are crocuses, daffodils, and bluebells", growled the creature, "All you have to do everyday is to push the bulbs up a little until they reach the surface of the ground underneath the forest, and in the spring they will break through the soil and blossom into lovely flowers". They looked at each other rather surprised, as it did seem to be in an excellent cause. The creature grinned showing chunky square-cut teeth, that looked nearly transparent. "I'm forgetting to introduce myself", he continued grinning again, "My name is Gelid", he said proudly, "It means frosty cold, and that's what I am, I'm in charge of the winter programme to encourage plant growth".

They stood huddled together wondering what was to come next. Bluey whispered to Greeny, "See his teeth, they look like clear mints you can buy in Mum's shop". Gelid growled under his breath, and looked intently at Bluey, "Do you think he heard me?", Bluey whispered again. "I shouldn't think so, or he'd probably eat you", replied Greeny. "Look I do believe he wants you to go first, he's pointing at you". Bluey edged nervously into the direction indicated, followed by the others; in the next room it felt quite warm, and in this ceiling were transparent oval shapes containing the beginnings of various warm blooded animals. "You see another important task", said Gelid, "It is essential that you feed them the correct amount of concentrated food each day, which you must propel through these tubes", he said, indicating a web made of a complicated fine mesh. "I didn't know animals started like that", said Pinky. "Of course they don't", Orangey spoke barely audibly, "there's something peculiar going on here".

In the next chamber it felt extremely cold again, and here they were shown microscopic fishes swimming in glass tanks, with narrow funnels running out of the sides and leading into the walls. "Now again these specimens must be fed with even greater care", rasped Gelid, and crunching his blunt teeth together like a rat trap snapping closed. "The least fungi infection accidentally introduced could kill them all within minutes", his aggressive manner threatened to turn into violence at any time, then in a twinkling he changed. "Before I show you the other tasks, we'll go to the banqueting hall, where we have a feast ready for you. It's not all work you see". He started to grin, but when Bluey sniggered loudly, he changed in a flash, suddenly producing a curved dagger which he swished through the air in a sweeping arc. "Only to carve the meat with", he grated, as they fell back in alarm. "Follow me", he commanded, and stalked into the passageway leading back to the area where they had started from.

They all trooped after him, and as they entered the massive cavern they could see that it had been transformed, a red glow shimmered from concealed lights above, illuminating a slowly revolving ice glacier, packed with dishes of marvellous foods. On the level surface were cold succulent red salmon, with an assorted mixture of salads on green crystal salvers, dressed crab decorated with shells filled with oyster meat, and giant prawns standing in tumblers garnished with lemon slices. Then amazingly on the same ice cold surface, were dishes of bubbling hot crimson lobster, with a separate spicy sauce, alongside a huge rib of roast beef, with fluffy Yorkshire pudding, and crispy roast potatoes, all kept hot on a bed of glowing coals, that by some magic, didn't melt the ice table. The choice was tantalising, but so were the selection of almond pastries and chocolate cream gateaux; with a centrepiece of a fantastic trifle nearly a foot high, and sprinkled with green angelica and red cochineal, covered with thick dairy cream, that flowed over the surface, out into a whipping machine and then back again, becoming creamier and smoother than ever.

Bluey just couldn't resist it, he picked up a spoon and scooped up a great mouthful covered in lovely rich cream, as he popped it into his mouth, the flowing cream changed shape, and replenished the hole in the trifle making it whole and untouched. "Cripes", mumbled Bluey, "I'm going to like it here", and took another huge mouthful, and then raised his spoon to dig in once more. Out of the corner of his eye he spotted Gelid who brandished his dagger and then expertly began to slice the beef. They were all fascinated by the revolving cycle of food, and forgetting their desperate position, helped themselves to everything that was on display. Gelid continued to wield his dagger wherever it was needed, and chopped and sliced his way through salmon and lobster, beef and pudding. Would you believe that after every single helping was taken, it was automatically replaced, the same as Bluey's first helping of trifle had been. As they gobbled up the delicious food, Orangey suddenly stopped eating and shouted out, "I've got it I think; no plants or animals begin their lives in tanks underground, I believe that the Ice Queen has a plan to cover the forest with poisonous plants, and invade it with infected animals, so that she can gain control of it. She's probably in cahoots with Haggotty the witch". They all stopped eating and looked at Orangey in horror. "You really think that is possible?", they asked. Before he could respond, the ice cavern began to revolve, faster and faster it spun, doors and windows opened and closed in the walls, strange faces leered out at them, grimaced and disappeared from view; the lights above flashed on and off, giving out a deepening blood coloured hue, and finally the music started again, swelling in volume, and culminating in a loud crescendo of noise that left them feeling dizzy, until one by one they fell to the ground and lost consciousness.

The next thing they all vaguely remembered was being transported through the air, and reaching a solid ice mound, with individual cells built into it. They were popped in one by one, and the glazed ice doors frozen into position, so that they were trapped inside. Slowly they regained consciousness, but sat staring out through the slightly transparent doors as though in a trance. Feeling colder and colder they realised that the Ice Queen was making good her threat to intern them in ice forever, if they refused to join her kingdom.

The brothers and fairies tried to make out the cell which held Orangey and Goldie, willing them to create some magic to release them, but Orangey and Goldie were staring back at them unable to help in their semi-frozen state. As they shivered and began to freeze into solid blocks of ice, they heard the Queen's voice speaking to them from somewhere above, "Anyone who wants to join us can agree to sign my royal decree, and will be released immediately. As for the others, as soon as you reach fifty degrees below zero you will be left in limbo for ever", she paused, and added, "Sign now or become a frozen Zombie, you have no other alternative".

Their failing eyes could just make out a shape moving in the corridor, it was Gelid carrying a parchment, he held it up in the entrance of each cell as he slithered by; he stopped in front of Bluey's cell, and grinned showing his chunky clear mint teeth, "Not so funny now, am I? Only I can save you". His voice croaked, and he coughed, and waved the parchment, "Just sign here", he said pointing to the bottom of the page, "There are over a thousand others who have already signed; they can't all be wrong". Bluey stared straight ahead, "I'll give you an especially heated pen to warm your hands", added Gelid, producing a long tube with a white feather on one end, and glowing red tip on the other. Bluey's eyes flickered, "Changing your mind at last", chided Gelid. Bluey gazed across the corridor and saw Orangey's eyes blink three times, Gelid stopped waving the document, his arms slowed and became rigid, he opened his mouth to speak, but it stayed open, not a sound coming out, he was rooted to the spot. Orangey blinked again and again, until the ice doors began to melt.

Goldie was the next out of her cell and they sped up and down the corridor, ensuring that all of the doors were melting and releasing their prisoners. "Phew I was getting worried", said Bluey, "I wondered if you were ever going to get us out, or even if you could". "Well in sub-zero temperatures it was really difficult", admitted Orangey, "It was not until Goldie and I managed to lock eyes that we could generate enough magic power, I just couldn't have managed it alone". "Why Orangey, you've never admitted before that I helped you", sighed Goldie. "Really", Orangey replied, "perhaps I've never said it, but I've always known about our combined powers and appreciated your help". Goldie smiled and lowered her eyes. "Well what shall we do now?", she asked, "we still have to find a way of escaping from this dreadful place". "I've been thinking how best to do just that", mused Orangey, "How would you all like to have a mass of those crazy blue crystals on your heads?". "What", said Greeny, "No thanks". "Don't worry I'll be controlling them not the Queen", countered Orangey. "How about him?", asked Goldie, pointing to Gelid, standing there as stiff as a ramrod. "He's already got crystals on his head controlled by the Queen". "True", said Orangey, "but if I blink like this into his eyes, I'll take over, and the Queen will not realise until it's too late, I hope" he added.

Within a few minutes Orangey's powers had created wriggling blue crystals on all of their heads including his own. "Feels pretty weird, just like a pot of worms crawling about all over you", said Pinky. "Yes we know", they all agreed, "pretty weird".

Orangey looked intently into Gelid's face, the stony eyes moved, his eyebrows slightly, and the evil eyes glazed over and became vacant. Orangey demanded in a loud voice, "Open up in the name of the Queen", the door swung open as the crystals on the guard's head spluttered loudly and then exploded, and he fell to the ground motionless.

They hurried into what was an outer guardroom, and then held their breath, sitting there were a group of fearsome animal warriors. They looked up sourly, slowly getting to their feet and growling menacingly. Most were armed with short blood spattered swords, and black nailed clubs, covered with brown spots of dried blood, and they carried round shields of glinting metal in front of them.

Without warning they roared and charged, Orangey managed to blink three times, and Goldie just twice, the weapons dropped from the animals' grasp, their shields clattered on the ground, and their clubs spun round in their useless arms, and attacked the warriors until they fell to the ground. Foam formed on their gaping mouths, and green sweat poured from their gruesome faces. Orangey and Goldie blinked yet again, and the warriors staggered up and grabbed their weapons and stood in a forlorn bunch, as though waiting for orders. Orangey nodded and blinked at them, and they rushed in a mad horde into the corridor, uttering blood curdling screams as they stampeded in the direction of the Queen's chamber.

Breathing with relief, Orangey and the others soon discovered three long and winding corridors leading away from the guardroom, and in it were more solid ice doors. They opened the first one and found a tall pixie who had been frozen but was reviving fairly quickly, he had a golden brown face, with a big smile, and he told them to follow him as he knew where the more important prisoners were kept.

Firstly they passed separate cells containing gnomes, pixies, tiny fairies, dormice, squirrels, rabbits, and other innocent animals trapped by the Queen and her henchmen. These were released, and followed the group to the next turning. As the ice doors were melted to release the occupants, great pools of water were beginning to collect on the floor, getting deeper by the minute. The tall pixie, groped under the water, and with a great effort pulled open a trap door, water and melting ice cascaded down the steps leading to a dungeon below, down which they had to tread very carefully.

The pixie led the way, his huge eyes shining out into the darkness, creating beams of light as they made their way further underground. "I wonder if we are getting to the centre of the earth", whispered Bluey, "I doubt it, I should think there are several more miles to go", replied Pinky, "and it's certainly not getting any warmer".

The Pixie stopped at the next door, and peered in through the hatch, his eyes lighting up the whole cell. "Look at this", he instructed. Orangey and Goldie looked in and couldn't believe their eyes. Sitting there was a beautiful girl dressed in rags; her tears had frozen into droplets. "Why she looks just like Cinderella", said Goldie. They opened the next hatch and gazed in, "Look this must be Peter Pan and Wendy together", said Orangey, "I can see his wings quite clearly". Further on they thought they spied Jack and Jill, then an old fat woman who looked like Mother Goose, she puffed out her feathers and offered them an egg. "I wonder if it's gold", asked Bluey following up behind. In the next cell was Aladdin frozen in the act of rubbing his lamp. "You know I can't guess what he did to upset the Queen", said Orangey blinking his eyes.

Out came Widow Twanky, Jack Whittington and his cat, and many others. "Do you know", suggested Goldie, "I do believe that somehow she has captured all the pantomime characters, so that there will be none able to play at the Theatres this Christmas".

When they reached the final door they opened it without looking in, and as the door melted, a huge leaf then another, and then a twig, followed by a branch and more and more branches and leaves grew out rapidly into the corridor filling it up. They let out a cry of alarm. "What's going on, there'll be no room to move if it gets any bigger". From inside a voice with a distinct country twang, shouted out, "Here help me direct it through the roof", Orangey looked in, "Where are you?", he said, "Here on the top" replied the country voice, and there perched on the top was a youth dressed in old fashioned country yokel's garb.

"Why I do believe it's Jack and his beanstalk", said Goldie, struggling to get in the door. "You're right lass, and the only way out of here is for my beanstalk to grow up through the roof, then we can climb up it and get out". So they all began to squeeze through the doorway and help Jack press the beanstalk against the dungeon's roof. Within seconds it had broken through and was rapidly growing upwards and outwards, with more and more branches appearing. Now there was room for everyone to begin climbing to safety.

"Yuk", said Bo-peep as she caught her dress on a twig. "My slippers have fallen off", cried Cinderella, "Don't worry", said Bluey, "I've got them". "Think I'm a duck?", grumbled Mother Goose as she waddled through the rising water, and mounted the bottom of the beanstalk. "I think my lamp's going to rust", complained Aladdin. "Now stop moaning all of you and climb faster, there's many others to come", urged Orangey.

Up they climbed and in a surprisingly short time they reached the top, and emerged from the ground by the lake. The stalk however continued to grow, up it rose, 30 and then 40 feet into the air. Bluey, Greeny and Pinky all held on tight and were soon miles above the ground. "Wow this is fun", they shouted, "It's like being on the Big Wheel at the fair". "You three had better come down before you do something silly, and fall off", said Goldie. Grinning happily they launched themselves into the air, sailed down flapping their wings, and blowing the light snowflakes into gusts of white powder. As they landed safely, and the last prisoners scrambled out of the Ice Kingdom, they heard a loud gurgling and rushing sound of water, and then a massive stream jetted out of the ground near them, and shot a column of water into the air like a giant oil gusher. As they looked up expecting to be drenched at any moment as the water fell back, it suddenly froze into a gigantic icicle. Gazing in horror they saw trapped in the ice, many grim faced creatures, and Gelid with his features set in a permanent snarl, and right in the centre was the Ice Queen, her face blue and still contorted with rage, surrounded by the animal warriors with their weapons raised. In seconds there was a tremendous crack, and the ice column toppled over, and plunged into the lake, spearing the ice and sliding rapidly from view.

They stood there holding their breath, "Well that's that", said Orangey. "There's only one last thing to do, and that is to get everyone home in one piece". He blinked his eyes and there in the middle of the forest, suddenly appeared a magnificent golden coach, with six black manned snorting horses. "There, that's the only traditional way for pantomime characters to travel", announced Orangey.

Cinderella clapped her hands with glee, "It's beautiful and much bigger than mine, I'm sure we can all squeeze in", she said. Then with much pushing and shoving, the pantomime characters clambered in, and after some shouting and argument, as to who should sit where, and with whom, they were all ready to go. The coachman cracked his whip, the horses whinnied, and reared, and then galloped away heading through the wood, accompanied by much waving and shouts of "Thank you", "Yes we'll be careful", "Come and see us in the Pantos", "We'll leave free tickets at the door".

At last all the noise and confusion sank into the distance, and the forest returned to its usual quiet and calm. "You know it's lucky that the pantomime people don't all appear together in one show", said Goldie, "I'm sure that they'd never agree to anything". "Ah well, thank goodness they've all gone", said Bluey, "By the way does anyone fancy coming ice skating again tomorrow night?". What they all replied shall for ever remain a secret, but it did bring a blush to the face of the Happy Gnome who was returning from giving the fox his repaired coat, to ask who had won the race across the lake.

ORANGEY AND THE
TRAVELLING CIRCUS

There was great excitement in the village, as a travelling circus was planning to visit a nearby town only five miles away. It was scheduled to remain for three whole days, giving everyone in the neighbourhood every opportunity of going.

When Orangey and his brothers left school late in the afternoon they saw posters advertising the circus plastered all around the village. Some were even stuck on telegraph poles, with others on shop windows and bus stops, seemingly everywhere.

On passing the village store where their Mother worked most afternoons, Bluey pointed to a large sized poster in the window. It showed the exact days when the circus would be playing, and featured some of the main acts appearing.

"Look", exclaimed Pinky, "reforming lions and a trapeze act", he quickly added, "It's the Andretti family we saw on television last Christmas". "What do you mean reforming lions?", Bluey chided, "You mean performing lions".

Pinky's face became darker, "Of course it's performing lions, I was only joking", he retorted, and pulled off Bluey's cap and flung it into the air, trying to lodge it onto the telephone wires, but it fell off. "You'd jolly well have had to get it back, if it had stayed there", Bluey complained. "Yes he'd have to tightrope along the wires", sniggered Greeny. "Some chance", Bluey said, "he'd fall off in no time".

Orangey interrupted their silly chat, "I remember now, I think Pinky's right, the Andretti's trapeze act is famous all over the world, and there is a midget who appears with them, and performs incredible stunts. We must try and go, let's ask mum".

The boys tore home, racing each other down the street, and crashed noisily into the cottage, forgetting that their parents were both still at work. So they dashed upstairs to the bedroom, and hastily removed their school uniforms. Grinning with delight, they set about becoming clowns, with bright red noses, and outrageous mouths created with red Crayola pens. One pretended to be a lion tamer, with black moustache and beard, the other became the ringmaster, with black pencilled eyebrows and smoothed down slick hair.

There was a fair old noise going on in the house when their Mother reached home. Before she could remove her coat, she was besieged by a junior clown, a lion tamer and the ringmaster. "You are awful", she said, "I hope you haven't been at my make up", she added. Looking anxiously at the black moustaches, and varying colour red noses. "Of course not, we used Orangey's old paint box". They jumped up and down with excitement, "What do you think Mum? We'd make good circus people". "I'm not sure about that", she said, fumbling in her purse, "but look I've got four tickets, front row seats for Thursday night". They all clustered around her excitedly, "Where did you get them?" they demanded. "This afternoon a clown came into the shop and asked if he could hang a large poster in the window". She smiled, "Mr Clements the owner said he could, and we were given the tickets". She giggled herself at the exclamations of glee. "Well Mr Clement's children are grown up, so he gave them to me".

Wednesday at school passed very slowly, and Thursday absolutely crawled by. Orangey only just stopped himself from making a magic spell so that Thursday would arrive immediately. He knew it was silly as eventually the time came to set off to the circus. They got off the bus and could see the circus Big Top with its myriad of flags and streamers fluttering in the wind, transforming the recreation ground behind the Town Hall. As they mingled with the crowds they could clearly hear the low growls of the lions nearby. "They sound very fierce", Pinky said worryingly.

Then one roared loudly which started the others raising a sinister throaty sound. There was a crack of a whip and it became strangely quiet. "I hope the cage is strong", shivered Pinky. "Of course it is or they wouldn't let us in", Greeny reasoned. "Let us in!", said Bluey, "We don't have to go into the cage do we?". "In the circus, not in the cage", replied Orangey. "I knew that really", said Bluey.

"Why have you gone all white in the face then?", joked the others. "Oh no I haven't", "Oh yes you have", the others insisted.

"You know Pinky, now you've gone very pale", kidded Bluey. "They wouldn't let us in if it wasn't safe, would they?" queried Pinky. "What do you mean, they don't let us into the cages", chided Bluey. "Into the circus, you know what I meant", screamed Pinky, pulling off Bluey's cap in revenge, and kicking it to Greeny. Greeny missed it, and it fell into the tub of murky water, Pinky snatched it out, and thumped Bluey on the back of the head with the smelly soggy cap.

Before their childish antics continued, they were suddenly distracted by a huge grey elephant loping by, followed in single file by several others. His massive tusks were yellowed with age, and blunted like giant hockey sticks, and holding onto his skinny tail by its trunk was a slightly smaller elephant with extra large hairy ears. After it there was another, again slightly smaller, followed by several others, all getting smaller by degrees. Coming up the rear, trotted a baby elephant with a strange blue tinge colouring his mottled skin.

He wasn't holding onto the tail in front of him, and coiled his tiny trunk in the air trumpeting shrilly. The leading members of the file ambled on ignoring his naughty behaviour, but as he walked by, he craftily stuck his trunk into the pail of dirty water, and sprayed it over the elephant directly in front of him.

"Did you see that cheeky little one?", asked Pinky, but before there was an answer, the elephant with big hairy ears, strolled over and lifted the baby easily with its trunk. Then with a quick flick, deposited him into a mound of grubby used sawdust of doubtful origin. He scrambled up, blowing the sawdust out of his trunk, and trumpeting shrilly in annoyance, hurrying to catch up with the rest, as they swayed into the "Big Top", and disappeared from view.

The evening's entertainment was unbelievable, the brilliant laser searchlights beamed onto each act separately, the extraordinary lighting showing them at their amazing best. They found it difficult to decide who were the most entertaining. They had witnessed beautiful white horses, with red and shining black plumes on their heads, gallop around the ring at an incredible speed, while their dainty rider stood on their backs, and leapt from one to another with surprising agility. She then ushered them out of the ring, retaining one great snorting black stallion, which she rode like a Cossack, passing under its belly as it careered around at top pace. Finally she balanced on its back, and fired a pistol, shooting out six lights with six shots, and then galloped out of the ring clearing the barrier with one tremendous stride. The applause continued for minutes, and was still ringing out when the clowns came tumbling into the centre of the ring.

Soon they were shouting out funny remarks to the crowd, as they played tricks on each other, and threw buckets of water at random. Almost unnoticed some of the biggest ones were cleverly assembling a steel cage, finally trapping the smallest ones inside.

After much whip cracking, and jeers, and cries of encouragement from the audience, they managed to escape by running down the corridor where the animals usually entered.

No sooner had the midget clowns left, several roaring tawny lions charged into the cage and clawed at the sides. The lion tamer with an exaggerated bow to the audience, strode into the centre of the cage without a whip, and stood there defying the lions with sheer power of will.

After a few moments a movement at the side of the cage revealed a small figure who had been sitting quietly on a stool watching the lions. He rose up and presented a whip to the lion tamer, who smiled down at him, and took the whip in his hand. Then with a flick of the wrist he put the aggressive beasts through their routine, he was impervious to the snarled and roared threats. He got them to pose on stools, leap over barriers, and jump through burning hoops, all without a word.

The small person on the stool, stood up again in full view of the lions, who paused in their antics and roared in his direction. One stalked over, and roared right into his face, he didn't waver; it then opened its mouth into a gaping hole, studded with sharp cruel fangs.

The brothers were sitting in the front row, closest to the animals, and could hardly believe the size of the beasts close up. Their huge pads hid the steel of the claws, the muscles of their legs and necks, standing out in huge gleaming ripples. But the eyes fascinated them, deep and brown, with orange and yellow flecks, brimming and cunning, waiting to take advantage of any error of judgement by their tamer.

They held their breath as the tiny figure coolly climbed onto a stool, with the lion hovering over him. He slowly raised his head until it had completely disappeared into the lions gaping mouth. The audience gasped, worried by the slightest movement ... the seconds ticked by, then a cry of relief went up from the watching crowd as the midget figure, expertly somersaulted off the stool, and waved out smiling to the worried audience.

There was another crack of the whip, and the lions dived down the narrow corridor, and out into their permanent cages. Immediately a host of clowns rushed into sight, and expertly began to dismantle the cage. Some were already playing tricks on each other again, and throwing buckets of water at the audience, who screamed and turned away, but amazingly the water changed into coloured confetti.

The same tiny clown who had been in the lions' cage, returned unexpectedly driving a vintage car. He was dressed in Edwardian driving clothes, which hung to his feet making him look even smaller. In no time he had the children in fits of laughter as everything possible started to go wrong with the car.

Firstly the doors and lights fell off, then the side wings, and then suddenly steam poured out of the radiator, and the bonnet flapped up. One tall clown with a crimson red nose, and big green feet, jumped on and tried to keep the bonnet down, but of course he fell and chased the car hopelessly, never catching it up, and shaking his fist as it zoomed by him. Then the car turned and chased him, threatening to run him over at any moment. Eventually the seats fell off, leaving just the engine and four wheels.

Finally it careered to the side, where the tyres fell off and it sped on, running on the hubs until it crashed into the barrier, with its horn hooting, and despite all efforts wouldn't stop.

Some of the bigger clowns picked up the pieces of the car, and carried them out of the ring, holding the little clown upside down in their arms. But he kept running back in to take yet another bow from the crowd. Four or five times he was carried out and dumped only to return, so finally they placed him on a white pint-sized pony, who trotted off with him facing the wrong way.

The excitement died down for a while as the house lights came on, and attendants passed up and down offering ice-cream, soft drinks, popcorn and chocolate. During the end of this period a buzz arose from the crowd as the trapeze was seen being hoisted into position. Suddenly it went dark, and then the laser beams spotlighted the famous Andretti family high on the platforms above the audience.

Two dark husky young men, and three attractive scantily dressed girls waved out, and to a roll of the drums, began their routine of flying somersaults, diving and catching each other, the ever moving crossbars being caught with disciplined ease.

Without warning a small clown climbed rapidly up the rungs of the ladder, the spotlight picking him out as he reached the top of the highest trapeze. He deftly swung the crossbar out over the audience; nearly eighty feet above them, there was no safety net in sight. A roll of the drums set the music going, and he swayed backwards and forwards in time to the beat, which progressively became faster and faster.

The crowd began to clap in unison with the music enjoying the participation, when to their horror, he slipped. He fell helplessly downwards, and at the last second with brilliant timing caught the lower crossbar propelled out to him by one of the other acrobats. The ground seemed to be only inches away, as he swung in an upward arc, and then landed safely on the platform. After they had shrieked in alarm, the audience slowly realised that it was all part of the act, dangerous but brilliantly calculated.

Everyone clapped and shouted enthusiastically, as he turned head over heels from crossbar to crossbar, changing places with the girl acrobats at the last possible moment.

It was nearly too much to bear, everyone's heart beating with excitement throughout the entire spectacle. Finally it was over, and reluctantly they filed out of the Big Top, leaving the smell of the sawdust, the performers, the thrills, and the animals behind.

The brothers dawdled by the lions' cages, stopping to watch them being fed huge lumps of red meat, which they tore and ripped into, before bolting them down, still in good sized chunks.

Orangey was walking behind the others, pondering on the amount of effort that went into putting on such a spectacular show. Lost in thought, he paused before a cage, when without warning a dark black object sprang out of the shadows and landed on his back. The sudden shock and the impact made him lose balance and he fell to the ground, spluttering as the sawdust went up his nose.

He twisted around in alarm, and spied a hairy leg wrapped round his waist, and further up two muscular arms encircled his chest. Trying to regain his breath, to shout for help, he came face to face with the grinning white teeth of a baby chimpanzee, jabbering for all it was worth.

As he scrambled to his feet, the baby chimp grabbed his hand, and tried to lead him along between two of the animal cages. After a moment's hesitation, he allowed himself to be guided past some very colourful trailer homes, until they reached a much smaller trailer painted in red and white candy stripes.

The chimp let go of Orangey's hand, and sprang up to the window, hanging onto the awning with one hairy hand, and rapping on the window noisily with the other.

A white face appeared and looked out suspiciously, it was pale and gaunt with dark shadows under the eyes. The eyes themselves were green and bright, and stared out into the early evening gloom, slowly focusing on the baby chimp. Then they turned and set on Orangey, the face lit up into a faint but warm smile. A hand beckoned and the door to the caravan opened, and to Orangey's astonishment, the tiny dwarf stood there inviting him in.

On entering the caravan home, he realised that the dwarf was only about his own height, but somewhat heavier in build. The caravan was surprisingly comfortably furnished and equipped, the furniture obviously custom made, as it was about three-quarter normal size.

Orangey did not know whether to address him as a clown, an acrobat, or a lion tamer, but was soon put at ease by his charming manner.

He gestured for Orangey to sit down, and without asking poured him out a glass of cola, pushing it across the table. As Orangey sipped the cold drink, he wondered what the dwarf wanted to talk to him about.

In his quaint Italian accent he told Orangey that his name was Mario, and then opened a map of Italy, and pointed out a village in the south where he had been born. Orangey screwed round in the chair and read aloud, "Lucianos", "Si" Mario replied, "may I now explain to you the reason I had my little chimp friend bring you to see me".

He unfolded the story, of how he and his twin brother had been brought up in Southern Italy, in a remote area. He related that because of their lack of height, they had found it necessary to excel in whatever they did, and over the years they had perfected a series of acts that could be used in the circus. "Because of your lack of height?", queried Orangey. Mario shrugged his shoulders. "You know that people are inclined to judge by what they think is normal, not realising that we have to live in the same world as them, as small as we are". He continued with another shrug, "Now you've seen the show, you may have some idea how hard my brother and I had to work to achieve such perfection".

He offered Orangey another cola, and began again "While I was performing in the circus this evening, I felt a strange kinship with someone in the audience", he looked intently at Orangey, and said, "I believe it was you.

Orangey could only nod in quiet agreement. "Now", said Mario, "I'll come to the point, the reason for my asking you here is that I'm afraid that I have contracted a particularly nasty virus, which has weakened me, and I'm afraid that I shall not be able to continue my act for much longer".

He shrugged yet again, "I have tried to contact my twin brother in our home village, but because it is so remote, it may be several days before he arrives here". He looked out of the window at the chimp who was peering in, it poked out its tongue and jumped down out of sight. He managed a slight laugh, "I do believe that he is peeved with me for not letting him in, but he is such a distraction, when there is something serious to discuss". He coughed into his hand, and spoke again, "The problem is that although my brother can take over the act when he arrives, what happens in the meantime, as I don't wish to break our contract, you see in the meanwhile ..." he left the words hanging in the air, and looked at Orangey.

Orangey swallowed, "You mean I do your act. Is that possible? You said it took you years to learn". Mario smiled at last, he hesitated, "Yes, where we live in the secluded mountains strange stories of witches and fairies are still believed". He grunted, "The wicked ones are known to terrorise the countryside to this day, but we also have magic fairies and elves who do good, I think you are one of those". Orangey did not reply, so Mario continued, "I watched you carefully when I was in the lions' cage, and I'm sure you are more than just a normal small boy".

Orangey was surprised as never before had an adult suspected that he was anything else other than a small boy. He looked closely at Mario, and decided that he was an exception, and would honour Orangey's secret, to never divulge that in reality he was a 'magic elf'.

Orangey replied quietly, "I do have magic powers". Mario's face visibly brightened, "Do you think you could possibly stand in for me until my brother arrives?", he asked. Orangey nodded his head, "With instruction from you, and a little magic help, I think I can".

Orangey was very flattered that Mario had such confidence in him, and that evening he was shown all of the expertise and special tricks that Mario had developed since he was a boy in Italy.

Two hours or so later as Orangey left the caravan, he saw that the night had closed in, bringing a damp mist which shrouded the circus, making the sounds of the animals quite eerie and frightening.

As Orangey sped home he felt extremely excited and elated, he had promised to fly to the town where the circus was playing the following night, so he had much to consider.

He landed at the end of the street, and toddled home in the darkening night, lost in thought. Unusually his

Mother was anxiously waiting for him in the doorway of the cottage. "Where have you been?", she declared. Orangey gave a slight grin and said, "Sorry but I was watching the lions and missed the last bus, but I got a lift, although I had to wait until Mr Anson closed his garage". It was the best excuse he could think of, and he kept his fingers crossed that his Mum wouldn't be likely to see Mr Anson in the near future and thank him. She seemed relieved that he was OK and didn't mention it again as he ate his supper.

In bed that night his brothers were disappointed that Orangey did not want to go into details of what really happened after they left the circus. "Must be something quite special". whispered Bluey, "Crumbs he's asleep already", he added, as gentle snores echoed from Orangey's bed.

The following day was a Saturday, and from early morning Orangey disappeared into the wood on his own. During the day there was less chance of meeting the fairies, so when he was satisfied that no one was about, he blinked his eyes to create a magic formula, to help him. He then spent the next two or three hours swinging through the trees, stopping and starting and trying to judge distances accurately. Because of his many previous flights through the forest at night, heights were no problem to him. But after a while he did begin to feel like Tarzan in the jungle, and began to feel really confident in his ability.

Satisfied that he had attained a reasonable overall

knowledge of the art of trapeze, he flew home through the forest, and arrived just in time for lunch.

During the meal he casually mentioned to his Mother that he had been invited to the circus to view the animals in their cages, and watch them being fed and groomed.

As the circus was still only a bus ride away, she raised no objection, but cautioned him not to miss the last bus home again. So clutching his fare money he set off for the bus stop, making sure that no one was about, he blinked twice, and seconds later landed safely outside Mario's caravan.

Mario appeared to have been waiting for him, as he opened the door immediately, and ushered him in. "I'm so pleased to see you", he said, "I was afraid that you might have changed your mind".

Orangey grinned, "Of course I wouldn't change my mind, and I'm rather looking forward to it". "Good", breathed Mario with relief, and added, "Incidentally at your suggestion I've told the ringmaster that I shall be appearing in an orange coloured costume and mask, for the time being". Trying to raise his spirits, he smiled wanly, "I hope they think the colour suits me".

When the time to appear arrived Orangey took a deep breath, and bounded into the circus ring. The applause broke out immediately, as he went through all of the routines splendidly, including the difficult trapeze act.

True he had nearly missed the downward swing of the crossbar, and nearly gave everyone a heart attack, before with an unseen flap of his wings; he had regained height and luckily and thankfully clutched the bar.

The fun with the clowns on the falling apart car, had only been marred by one of the midgets, a French clown named Claude. He had deliberately tried to set fire to the seat of Orangey's elfin outfit. He was somewhat put out by this, as he did not remember it being part of the original set.

The time he had spent in the lions' cage was the most frightening, it had set his heart racing, when it was his turn to stand on the stool and place his head in the male lion's mouth.

The smell inside the mouth was terrible, like rotting meat, and he knew that if it closed its jaws, the teeth would remove his head as efficiently as the guillotine in the French Revolution.

However the lion was well trained, and behaved itself, so Orangey gratefully somersaulted off the stool, and took his bows, exactly the way Mario had shown him.

Later on back at the caravan, Mario was saying how delighted he was with Orangey's performance. Apparently he had remained out of sight at the rear of the Big Top, and had noticed only one or two slight errors, not visible to anyone else.

That was except Claude, the midget clown, who although they did not know it, had become suspicious of Mario's health, and was planning to take his place in the future.

It appeared that he had sneaked up to the caravan home, and overhead Mario and Orangey discussing the possibility of Orangey taking over his role. He had been watching Mario carefully, and convinced that his health was failing, was preparing to make a bid for the contract.

The following four evening performances went smoothly, Orangey managing to avoid being set on fire by the troublesome Claude. Orangey had found no difficulty in leaving home each evening, as his parents thought he was doing his homework and then going to bed early. However his brothers were under strict instructions to keep quiet about his absence.

On the Saturday following the start of Orangey's circus life, he left early to meet Mario secretly in his caravan as usual. Mario was becoming worried as he still had no news of his brother Angelo arriving. Although the week's rest had helped, Mario was still extremely ill and weak.

Another real worry was that the ringmaster was intending to alter the routine of the lions' cage act, and there was to he a dress rehearsal that very morning.

Orangey did not know what to expect as he shook hands with the lion tamer and affirmed he was happy to go along with any sensible changes. The lion tamer looked at him intently, before explaining how he proposed to improve the act.

He had agreed that Claude was to be in it as well, and that Orangey would appear to stray into the cage as though he was lost. And then the lions would surround him and growl ferociously, cutting off his avenue of escape. When the audience had become worried for his safety, Claude was to swing from the roof, and pluck him from their jaws.

Finally to make it appear especially dangerous, Orangey's head was to be lodged in the lion's mouth, and then snatched away at the last possible moment.

Orangey was somewhat reluctant at this final twist, but felt that he had to agree, to uphold Mario's reputation.

As the lions were released from their cages they came bounding down the corridor, unexpectedly lively, and somewhat out of hand. Nevertheless, Orangey strolled into the centre of the cage as planned, and was immediately confronted by the lions. Very quickly they surrounded him, snarling with a hitherto unknown rage.

There was a frightening pause, before Claude swung down on the rope, and cleverly picked Orangey up. He then thrust Orangey's head into the largest lion's mouth, but something alarmed him about Claude's eyes, which alerted him to blink at the lion. Its jaws closed over Orangey's head, the fangs came together, and closed only inches apart.

The beast's mouth became rigidly locked partly open, Orangey felt a hefty tug, and his ears scraped past the lion's fangs, as he shot soaring up into the roof.

"Near thing", shouted Claude, "lucky I was quick, I saved you". The lion tamer waved from the floor of the cage, "Well done lads", he bellowed, "I'll leave you Claude to put the animals away, I'm off to tell the circus manager that we have a new act".

When he had gone Claude swung down, and dumped Orangey in a heap on the floor. He picked up the lion tamer's whip, and cracked it at the male lion, "What's wrong with you", he shouted, "move you blighter", and then struck the animal with the whip.

Orangey blinked from his position on the floor, and the whip flew out of Claude's hand, at the same time the lion raised its head and roared loudly, and then lashed out at Claude.

Claude frowned and bent down quickly and picked up the whip, then waving it at the lion slowly backed out of the cage. When he reached the tunnel entrance, he quickly slipped craftily past the gate, and slammed it closed.

Still holding the whip he stalked down the tunnel, and away from the cage, laughing hysterically. "See if you can escape from seven hungry lions", he shouted as he strode out of view.

Orangey was at a loss, he could create some magic, and turn the lions into statues, but what if someone came in, or the lion tamer returned to ensure that Claude had carried out his instructions.

He couldn't explain that he was a magic elf, or that he had been standing in for Mario, or the whole plan would come to light. While he pondered, six of the lions encircled him, but remained a few feet away growling softly. The seventh, the huge male lion, shook its mane, snarled menacingly, and padded towards him. Orangey looked round the cage and realised that both doors were locked from the outside; there was no obvious escape route.

The lion gathered itself together ready to spring, and then launched itself at Orangey. Having no choice Orangey stood his ground, and blinked in the direction of the leaping lion. Halfway through its upward curve the lion seemed to strike an invisible barrier, and fell back on its haunches.

It crouched again, and sprung higher, this time it crashed heavily to the ground, and lay there with a baffled look on its face. Half-heartedly it tried once more, but after meeting the invisible force again, it lay down and rolled over purring like an overgrown pussycat.

The remaining lions relaxed and stopped growling, with a brief glance from Orangey, they took their places on the balancing stools.

There was a sound of clapping from the shadows of the tent, and Orangey saw Mario walking towards him applauding. "Mario", sighed Orangey, "I'm glad you've come, I feel OK now, but I need a friend to talk to".

Holding out his hand as he walked toward him, he replied, "I'm Angelo, Mario's brother, I've arrived at last from Italy. He deftly opened the door to the cage and entered, and clapped Orangey on the back. "You were magnificent, Mario told me you had unusual powers, and now I see what he meant".

"Am I glad to see you", Orangey blurted out, "I wondered

if you'd ever get here". "I live in a remote area, among wild mountains, I came as soon as the message reached me", replied Angelo smiling.

"Well now I'm here we can go and celebrate with Mario, and tell him about the new act, it looks too dangerous to add to the routine, I think we'll suggest that it is dropped".

Back at the caravan, they drunk a toast to Orangey in a smooth Italian wine that Angelo had brought with him. With fervent invitations to visit their home in Italy, a fistful of front seat tickets, and their heartfelt thanks ringing in his ears, Orangey zoomed happily home.

He was well in front of the last bus, and felt relief to be able to return to school on Monday without problems on his mind. "Yes", he admitted to himself, "I'll be happy to go to school, and I'll even be pleasant to Miss Timson-Jones".

After all he was a normal small boy as well as a magic elf, and sometimes it was great just to play games with his brothers.

He reflected, "They'll want to know all about what I've been up to these last few days, I suppose I'll have to tell them the whole story or they'll never give me any peace.